I0760406

FRACTURED

THE ADOPTED SERIES
BOOK TWO

MEGGAN LARSON

Library and Archives Canada Cataloguing in Publications.

For permissions contact:

hello@starfishstoriespublishing.com

E-Book ISBN: 978-1-990419-27-0

Print ISBN: 978-1-990419-26-3

Hardcover ISBN: 978-1-990419-28-7

Dust Jacket ISBN: 978-1-990419-68-3

1st Edition

Edited by C.B. Moore

Cover Designed by Meraki Cover Design

To my fellow fractured adoptees. May we continue to piece ourselves back together.

1

I couldn't get my racing heart under control, and I had never felt my legs burn that way before. My lungs cried from the sheer agony of expanding and contracting at the pace I demanded. My arteries, I'm sure, were about to snap.

One foot in front of the other; my feet pounded against the rubber while my t-shirt clung to my skin, held there by the gallons of sweat pouring off me. I was surprised that I hadn't evaporated into thin air, having lost all my moisture on the track. I trailed behind half the team, which wasn't my usual place, or one that I particularly enjoyed occupying. The comforting smell of the track mixed with grass had been replaced by the sweat of the runners ahead of me. That was reason enough to push myself harder, but it seemed that no matter what I did, I was unable to catch up.

This team was different. They weren't high school students forced into running because of gym class. Everyone on this team had fought for their spot, and they weren't about to slack off.

"Pick up the pace, Olivia! You can do better than this."

Coach Addison yelled at me from the sidelines of the track. I nodded as I internally ordered myself to run faster, like a jockey whipping his horse.

I rounded the last bend of the track and clumsily dragged myself along, gasping for air. The worst part was that I wasn't out of shape; they were just better runners.

This is what you wanted, Liv. My eyes burned from the sweat cascading into them. I crawled across the finish line and immediately moved over to the grass. I sucked in as much air as I could while I bent over with my hands on my knees. The cramp in my side worsened with every breath I took. I jammed my hand into my ribs to alleviate the pain, but in vain. Out of the corner of my eye I could see Felicity Marcelli strolling toward me. I stood up and did my best to keep my breathing under control.

"Tough run out there, huh?"

I nodded, knowing I couldn't form a coherent sentence yet. Her black hair was pulled back into a tight ponytail and her cheeks had a faint glow to them. She hardly looked winded at all, even though she had come in first. As usual. *How is it she doesn't even break a sweat, while I look like I was tossed in a pool?*

My stomach was starting to hurt from forcing myself to breathe slowly and act like I wasn't about to pass out.

"Jackson, what's the deal?" Coach Addison was behind me, his tone as cutting as ever.

I turned slowly to look at him while Felicity mouthed *good luck* and began a light cool-down jog.

"What…do…you…mean?" I sucked in air between each word.

"Coach Stewart told me that you were the best. Do you feel like the *best* right now?"

His dark bushy eyebrows creased together, forming a long line across his forehead resembling a giant caterpillar. If I hadn't been in so much pain, I might have laughed. He folded his arms, wrinkling the jacket on his black elite track suit. I shook my head soberly. *No, I do not feel like the best. Quite the opposite, actually.*

I missed Coach Stewart. He had always been so encouraging. Coach Addison was a slave driver, constantly lashing out at me with his criticisms.

Was he ever going to stop picking on me? After four months of running for the Lion's Track Team, I thought the new-kid hazing would have worn off by now. I had been so happy to make the team in January, considering everything that had happened last year, but now I was on the verge of tearing off my black and gold jersey and walking away. My legs were shaking so badly under the pressure of my weight that it was a wonder they did not spontaneously detach themselves from my body just to get a break.

"You're not giving it your all out there." He gestured to the track and went on, "Felicity is running circles around you and she's *younger*." His hazel eyes were full of disapproval. Did he think I was unaware that she was younger? He brought it up nearly every practice.

"I'm…sorry."

I could feel it coming. The team had warned me that first week, but I had managed to avoid it—until now. Coach Addison was still talking at me, only I couldn't hear what he was saying anymore. All I could hear was the sound of my vomit escaping my mouth and falling on the grass inside the track. I was mortified even as I continued heaving.

"That's more like it, Jackson."

Coach Addison clapped me on the back, making me heave again, and blew his whistle, signaling the end of practice. I wasn't sure why, but he sounded *proud* of me for once. I smiled to myself for a second before losing the rest of my lunch.

"It couldn't have been *that* bad." The horror in Mela's voice betrayed her.

"You know full well you would have died if it were you," I said as I absentmindedly scrolled through my birth mother's Instagram feed.

She pretended to think about it for a moment and then grimaced. "You're right, I'd never show my face again."

I threw a red pillow at her from across the room, and she expertly dodged it. She knew what to expect from me after fifteen years of friendship. We had been best friends from the moment we crawled to each other in a playgroup our mothers attended. With the exception of a year she spent in Canada with her family, we had always been inseparable.

We'd been occupying her living room for the better part of an hour, sprawled on the buttercream carpet with her untouched homework beside her. Since we no longer attended the same high school, we made more of an effort to hang out during the week.

There were new pictures of my sister Leah on Ali's feed, and I found myself longing to reach out to her but feeling the immediate brick wall I knew was between us. It was impossible; if I ever wanted to be accepted by Ali, I had to play by her rules.

"Olivia, what a nice surprise."

Mela's mom sauntered into the room and sat down on the smooth brown leather couch.

"Hi, Mrs. Moretti." I smiled.

"Renae, dear. I feel so old when you call me Mrs."

"You *are* old, Mom. Didn't you just get up from a nap?" Mela teased.

"Honestly, Carmella. If I'm old, it's because *you* have aged me."

I grinned at their exchange. I never got to banter like that with my parents—it would be considered the height of rudeness. Renae had the same green eyes and flowy dark hair as Mela. Hers had gray roots, and I was positive she'd have them colored by the weekend. It was more disheveled than usual, and her familiar pinstriped jacket was wrinkled after her nap.

"How was track practice, Olivia?" Renae asked.

"It was positively *explosive*," Mela interjected, waggling her eyebrows at me before I could answer. I glared at her.

"It was…rough."

"Are you enjoying it, though?" she asked.

I thought about it. Was I enjoying it? No. It was harder than I thought it would be, and I felt like a failure.

"No, not really," I admitted. "I think I might throw in the towel."

"*Quit*?" Mela was incredulous. "After how hard you worked to get on that bloody team?"

I braced myself waiting for Renae's answer. I was secretly hoping she would agree with me and give me the validation I so desperately wanted. Instead, she said, "Carmella's right, honey. You can't quit."

"Why *not*?" I hated how I sounded like a whiny child.

"What good would quitting do? You would always look back on it with regret. Always wonder if you could have made it. Trust me, that's not a place where you want to live. Every decision you make in life will either take you closer to who you want to be or further away." She looked off wistfully and then seemed to collect herself.

"If you say so." I ran my fingers back and forth along the soft carpet.

I was disappointed. I had wanted her to tell me that of course I could quit. That no one expected me to continue doing something I had grown to hate. Practices were brutal, and the only kind of encouragement I had ever received from Coach Addison was today when I puked all over the grass. Was I really going to have to throw up three times a week to get his approval?

"What is this *really* about, Liv?" Mela's voice interrupted my thoughts.

Her mother had left the room while I was throwing my internal pity party. I gave her a sideways look and sighed.

"It's hard. Harder than I thought it would be. I hate every practice, and it's just not fun anymore."

"Is it because of Felicity?" she probed.

"No not entirely." I sat up, as I didn't even sound convincing to myself. "It's the whole team, really. They care so much about track, and I thought I did too, but I'm an amateur in comparison. It's like I just don't measure up anymore."

She grimaced sympathetically. Not being the best on the team was a position I wasn't used to, but feeling like I didn't measure up was very, very familiar.

I WALKED up my driveway and was surprised not to see my dad's work truck. He was usually home by now. I rifled through my purse for my keys only to remember that I had left them sitting on my desk in my room. *Damn.*

Changing course, I went through the side gate into our backyard. The motion sensor lights hadn't been working for a few months, so I hadn't expected to see the backyard revealed by a light in the house. As I approached, I saw that it was my mom in her office.

She was still in her work clothes, sitting at the desk with her head in her hands. I froze. A calculator sat to her right and a stack of papers was strewn around the desk. Whatever lay on that desk was causing her major stress. It felt strange to be getting a rare glimpse into my mother's life with her walls down. I didn't like it.

I made sure to give the window a wide berth as I walked up the deck and opened the back door. It was always unlocked.

"Mom? I'm home!" I called out.

"Hey, honey. I'll be up in just a bit. You ate at Mela's?" If I hadn't just witnessed her private stress, I wouldn't have been able to tell anything was wrong by the sound of her voice.

"Yeah, I did." I wrung my hands as I headed to the kitchen. *How long has she been stressed out like this?* I turned on the kettle absentmindedly and rinsed out the teapot. My mom loved tea. I grabbed two tea bags of Earl Grey—her favorite. Her light footsteps began coming up the stairs and I plastered a smile on my face before she could see my worry.

She came into the kitchen with sweats on and I stopped short of asking why she had changed. *Does she have a stash of emergency sweats or something?* I dropped the tea bags into the vintage teapot and poured the hot water into it, nearly overfilling it. I fastened the homemade green and yellow tea cozy she had made years ago and let the tea steep.

"You're making tea?" She sounded surprised.

I winced internally, wondering how long it had been since I did something thoughtful for my parents without being asked or prompted.

"I thought you'd like some."

Her eyebrow raise was further proof that I had been wrapped up in my own life for quite a while. I needed to be a better daughter.

"That's very thoughtful. Thank you, honey."

She squeezed my arm and headed to the living room. I followed her and sat on the beige couch with pink and blue swirls, making sure to avoid the cushion with the broken spring. I stole a glance at my mom as she sank into the burgundy loveseat and closed her eyes. Nothing matched in this house, but that was normal. So was her sitting on the couch after work with her eyes closed, but somehow it hit me differently today.

"Dad's working late again?" I tried to sound casual, but unease was starting to creep in. Was he working late all the time because they were struggling financially? Or in their marriage?

"Yes, he wanted to finish a few more jobs this week." She didn't open her eyes.

I nodded, though she couldn't see me. The lump in my throat was preventing me from speaking. I walked back into the kitchen and poured tea into her favorite mug. It was a wide-mouth ceramic one with a painted scene of the mountains. It had a chip in it but had been a gift from my brother, so it was likely never getting thrown out. I brought the tea back to the living room and placed it on the side table next to my—now sleeping—mom. It was getting dark out, so I turned on the porch light for my dad before heading downstairs.

The office was beside my bedroom, so I quickly snuck in and used the flashlight on my phone to illuminate the desk. I felt a tightness in my chest as my eyes caught more than one red-stamped overdue bill and a couple of FINAL NOTICE letters. I was right then. My dad was working overtime to try to catch up on bills. The lump in my throat was only growing bigger.

I tiptoed out of the office and into my bedroom, and sighed as my eyes fell on my unmade bed. I hurriedly tossed all the clothes on the floor into a hamper, added my track clothes to it, and went to the basement to turn on the laundry. I debated sending Mela a text about what I had just walked in on, but her parents were so well off… I found myself hesitating. I knew she wouldn't say anything, but I somehow felt like I'd be betraying my own parents' trust since they were actually friends with Mela's.

I sent Lucas a text instead. Maybe I was just overreacting.

After a brief shower, I headed to bed although it was still pretty early. My phone lit up as I was nestling into my covers.

> I'm so sorry. I've been there. It's not a fun thing to stumble across.

So, Lucas didn't think I was overreacting, then. Whatever was going on, I knew I'd have to be on my best behavior for a while. I couldn't and wouldn't add to their stress.

2

"Did you try this one?"

Lucas was gesturing to his computer screen at school. I glanced at it quickly, read the words *Biological Family Match* and shook my head no. We had been looking through websites for the past hour, trying to find some kind of clue as to who my birth father might be. Lucas had been helping me for months, but we were no closer to finding him than when we'd started.

"What about doing a DNA search?" he whispered.

"I don't have a hundred dollars to buy the kit. Plus, then my parents would know I'm searching."

I wasn't ready to tell them. Somehow, I didn't think my dad would be onboard this time around. I glanced miserably at the front of the room where my teacher, Mr. Masterson, reclined so far back in his chair that he seemed to perch precariously at the edge of a cliff. Only two of the four legs were touching the floor, his bright white sneakers were crossed at the ankle on his desk, and his Florida Panther's ballcap rested on his face to hide that he was, in fact, sleeping.

Maybe I'm just not meant to find my father.

"Don't do that." Lucas's voice gently broke into my thoughts.

I turned to him, and his hazel eyes bore into mine.

"Do what?" I mumbled as my eyes darted to the front of the room.

"Give up. I can see it in your face, but we're nowhere near done, Liv. We'll find him." He gently squeezed my arm, and I felt my heart skip a beat.

Even after months spending every day together, he still made my heart flutter with a single touch. I watched his fingers fly over the keyboard, typing quickly. His eyebrows creased as he focused on what he was reading. He ran a hand through his dirty-blond hair and reached for the mouse. He was wearing black shorts and my favorite turquoise hoodie. I loved the way it brought out the green ring around his irises.

"I can feel you staring at me, you know." The side of his mouth turned up into my favorite crooked smile, and heat rushed to my cheeks as I quickly turned away. I stared down at the rip in my jeans and played with the torn fabric.

I still wasn't sure why I was even looking for my biological father after the meeting with my birth mother had turned out so disastrous. *I'm sorry that I couldn't be who you needed me to be.* Her words replayed in my head often. Her rejection had burned a hole in my heart, and I didn't know if I would ever recover. Yet here I was, enlisting people's help to find my birth father, who might very well do the same thing. Deep down, though, I knew that what Lucas had said that night at Pink Lake was true. I really believed that I was going to save him somehow, so I couldn't stop looking.

"Hey, guys, I think I might have found something good."

Cara's excited whisper came from behind us. She had saved my butt in class at the beginning of the year when I was the new kid, and we had been friends ever since. She was tall, dark, curvy, and the kind of person who commanded a room just by entering it. We were basically opposites—but they say opposites attract, and it worked for us. I spun to look, and she was on her laptop at the round table behind us. I snuck another peek at Mr.

Masterson; since he was still sound asleep, I rolled my chair over to see what she had found.

"It looks like you can register on this site, and if your birth father has registered too, they'll match you and put you in touch."

My mouth turned to dust, and I rubbed my sweaty palms on my jeans to dry them. I swallowed hard as I stared at the blinking cursor daring me to enter my information. Lucas's hand on my shoulder made me jump in my seat. My knee slammed against the underside of the table. The three of us collectively held our breath as Mr. Masterson snored and shifted slightly in his seat. Cara shot me a calm-the-heck-down look, and I winced at the pain in my leg.

A few other students glanced up from their laptops to give us a dirty look, but the majority didn't even seem to notice. Likely because it was pretty early and most of the room was uncaffeinated. I was still getting used to the way things worked at Banting. An alternate school wasn't where I thought I'd end up, but I liked it. There were no bells or changing classrooms multiple times a day. We did one subject at a time and went at our own pace through workbooks. Many of us were studying different subjects in the same room, hence Mr. Masterson's slumber habits. He was available for questions, but we hardly ever had any. It turned out that high school wasn't all that difficult when you removed the constant disruptions, cliques, and mandatory hour requirements. I was set to graduate next year, and it couldn't come soon enough.

Lucas had returned to his seat at the class computer, wisely knowing when I needed some space. I took quick shallow breaths, and there was now a small pile of fabric on the floor and a widened rip in my jeans. It was a strange sensation to want something desperately and be terrified of getting it at the same time. Since Lucas and I had that conversation about looking for my birth father, I had been full of hope and dread in equal measure. It was sort of exhausting.

"Just text me the link and I'll take a look at it later," I managed to squeak out.

Cara raised an eyebrow so high it nearly touched her hairline, but she shrugged and copied the link to send me. I was expecting it, yet I still jumped when my phone buzzed in my pocket. I slowly rolled back to my spot with her eyes boring into my back. I knew she couldn't understand my hesitation; as I could hardly understand it myself, I decided to refrain from attempting to explain.

I spent the morning feigning interest in my math book as I absentmindedly answered the problems in my workbook.

Question one: "Classify this polynomial."

Hey, Dad. Ugh, no, I can't call him that.

Question two: "Find the degree of this polynomial."

Hi, Mr. Birth Father, sir…Seriously, Liv? He'd know you are an idiot immediately.

Question three: "Is this figure a polyhedron?"

Hi. I hope it's okay that I looked for you? Maybe you didn't want to be found…

I closed my eyes for a moment, squeezing them tightly. There it was. The question that had been swirling around my mind and heart for the past several months. What if he didn't want to be found? Could I survive another Ali encounter?

I opened my eyes and blinked rapidly to force back any tears. Lucas turned his head quizzically toward me.

"I can feel you looking at me, you know." I teased him. I heard him snicker, but I wasn't ready to look over yet. The sound of students collecting their things made me look at the clock on the wall with surprise. *Ten to one already?*

"Are you working this afternoon?" Lucas asked while grabbing his books.

"Nope, I have the day off." I wasn't sure whether I was grateful for that fact or not.

"Why don't you come over to Nate's in a few hours, after football practice? We'll just hang out. Adoption registries and biological parents are off the list of acceptable topics of conversation."

"That actually sounds amazing. You're sure you have time?"

Lucas had been helping Nate with some of his school projects since we'd found out he was close to flunking the entire semester. There were only a few weeks left in the school year for Nate to pull it together.

"Always," he mumbled into my hair as he pulled me close and kissed my left temple.

I breathed him in deeply and let my hand find his and interlocked our fingers. We strolled out to the parking lot and headed to our vehicles. My rusty red Dodge Aries was next to a shiny black truck. I cringed a little at the glaring difference between them. The truck was practically sparkling.

"Nate doesn't mind you borrowing his truck every day?" I was surprised that after all this time Nate was fine using his motorcycle for everything.

"Actually..." Lucas ran his hand nervously through his hair. I looked up at him expectantly. "Nate's parents bought this one for me."

My jaw dropped as I looked it over. Sure enough, there were slight differences from Nate's truck. Tinted windows, not a single scratch and different rims were the first things I noticed. I let out a low whistle.

"I know. I tried to stop them, but they said that since I was living there full time, they couldn't let me keep borrowing Nate's truck every day in case he needed it."

I smiled knowingly. It was the only way Lucas would have agreed to something so extravagant. Nate's family was loaded, so it seemed like the natural progression to having Lucas move in with them after he'd left home last year. Still, I was surprised that he hadn't mentioned it. He gave me a goofy grin and climbed into the driver's seat. I was still standing outside my car, gawking at his truck as he rolled the passenger window down.

"I'll see you at Nate's around five? That'll give me enough time to shower after practice."

"Uh-huh."

I nodded distractedly as I clambered into my car. He pulled out of his spot and raised his arm to wave at Cara, who was walking my way. I turned the key in the ignition as she came up to my window. She tapped on the glass impatiently and I manually wound the lever to open it. Her white and yellow polka-dotted dress was blowing in the warm October breeze.

"Are you going to fill it out?" she demanded.

There was no sense in acting like I didn't know exactly what she was talking about. "Yeah. Probably tonight."

"I'll expect an update."

She pointed her finger at me as though daring me to argue. I simply nodded and gave her a tight smile. I pulled out of the parking lot and watched her get smaller in my rear-view mirror.

Great. I guess I'm doing this then.

JUST AFTER FIVE, I pulled into Nate's oversized driveway and marveled at the house, as I always did. The exterior siding was white, and beautiful beige and brown stonework covered the front of the house. The double front door was a dark mahogany, and the floor-to-ceiling windows reflected the partially cloudy blue sky. It was gorgeous.

To my surprise, Lucas pulled up just as I was walking to the door. He jumped out of the truck and jogged to where I was standing.

"Practice run late?"

"No, I had something to do for Nate after." His eyes were missing their usual playful spark.

"You okay?" I placed my hand gently on his chest, noticing for the first time the purplish circles under his eyes. How long had they been there?

I was about to ask when the corners of his mouth turned up into a smile.

"I'm good now."

He leaned down and pressed his lips against mine. I let myself get lost in the moment as the kiss deepened and my purse dropped to the ground. My fingers wound around the back of his neck as his hands pressed against the small of my back and pulled me closer to him. Tingles shot up my spine; he ran his thumb along my jawline and kissed me with an intensity I had never felt from him before. It left me breathless.

"*Ahem.*"

I dropped my hands and jumped away from Lucas as Nancy Martin stood in the doorway.

"Will you be coming in for dinner, or should I have some furniture brought out for you?"

The smirk on her face and twinkle in her grey eyes let me know I was forgiven for making out on her porch. Heat flooded my cheeks as I sheepishly picked up my purse and snuck past Nate's mom while she playfully ruffled Lucas's hair.

I spotted Mela, munching on strawberries and whipped cream at the kitchen island across from Nate, and beelined it over to her. I took the stool beside her and helped myself to some strawberries.

"What are we doing tonight?" I asked with my mouth full.

Mela shot me a disgusted look. "Well, now that you're both finally here, wanna just play some pool? I can't stay late." She popped another strawberry into her mouth.

"It's not our fault. Lucas was off doing whatever errand Nate needed done."

"Errand—" Nate stopped short and seemed to think better of it. "Right; sorry, I totally forgot. Thanks again, man."

"Sure, no sweat," Lucas replied easily, and again ran his thumb down my cheek, leaving a trail of sparks.

What was I about to say? I couldn't remember. I found myself staring at the two-day-old stubble on his face and had to stop myself from reaching for it.

Nancy took the strawberries and whipped cream away and shook her head at us. I glanced over and caught Mela's eye. She pretended to fan herself and I again felt my cheeks flush in embarrassment.

Dinner was steak fajitas, and they were delicious. I loved having dinner at Nate's place. His parents always had the best food. After dinner, Mela had to leave.

"Go? It's like six thirty. I thought we were playing pool?" It was shocking to see Mela heading home early.

"I know, I know. My dad just sent a text. I've gotta help my mom." She held her hands up in surrender.

"How is your mom?" Nancy was leaning against the wall in the doorway as Mela grabbed her things.

"Tired." She pursed her lips.

"Aren't we all?" Nancy laughed.

I could tell Mela was annoyed, and something in her eyes made me promise myself I would text her when I left.

"Want to hang out in my room?" Lucas murmured into my ear, low enough that no one else heard it.

I nodded and waved goodbye to Mela as I linked my fingers with his. We walked down the wide hallway, past Nate's room, which was relatively tidy except for the candy wrappers everywhere. Lucas's room was at the end of the hall, after two additional spare bedrooms, and it was massive. If I hadn't seen the rest of the rooms in the house, I'd think Nate's parents were giving him special treatment, but they were all huge. He left the door open as usual—his own personal rule to make sure he didn't get "carried away." I nestled into the corner of the bluish gray sectional couch and he snuggled in beside me.

He busied himself choosing a show for us to watch. "Do you want to talk about seeing your mom last night?"

I sighed. I didn't want to talk about it, but I also kind of did. "It really freaked me out. I thought my parents were fine."

Lucas put his arm around me and squeezed my shoulder. "I remember the first time I found my mom crying about money. When I tried to comfort her, she screamed at me for eating too much all the time."

"She *blamed* you?" I couldn't believe it. Mothers didn't do that, did they?

He smirked in response. I let out my breath and shook my head. Mela's parents were too functional, and Lucas's mom was the height of dysfunction. *Maybe I should keep my issues to myself.* We watched a few episodes of a comedy—trying and failing to lighten the mood—and then I called it a night.

At least the evening had done one thing: I hadn't thought about my birth father once.

LATER THAT NIGHT, after saying goodnight to my parents, I messaged Mela to make sure she was okay. She sent me a slew of emojis, annoyed that she had had to cut her night short when her mom was sleeping by the time she got home. But she assured me she was fine.

Since that was out of the way, I opened a browser on my laptop and hesitantly typed in the link Cara had sent me. It felt like a lifetime had passed since this morning, but I knew Cara would give me crap if I didn't register.

It felt more official, doing it on my laptop versus on my phone. I filled out the information requested as best I could, including Ali's name, my birthdate, and the city and hospital where I was born. Knowing half of my history did come in handy at times. I held my breath as I clicked the submit button.

A confirmation e-mail has been sent to you.

The words popped up on my screen and sent my heart fluttering. I quickly closed my laptop, sent Cara a text back to let her know the deed was done, and crawled under my covers. Conflicting thoughts swirled in my mind. I knew I should be focusing on my parents and what might be going on with them but filling out the registry had brought my birth father to the forefront of my mind.

What if he registered too and we get matched? The thought made my breath catch in my throat. I let it out slowly as a much more sinister thought took over.

What makes you think he registered at all?

3

It was busier at Brew than usual. I didn't mind the hustle; it just made the shift go by faster. Brew had been my after-school job for the last year, and it was a great place to work. I liked the laid-back atmosphere and having hundreds of books to flip through on slow days.

It had taken me weeks to be able to get back to work after everything that happened with Lucas and Chris last year. My psychopath ex-boyfriend's stalking of me blew up in a confrontation between him and Lucas in the parking lot by my work. Even now I still avoided looking out the window after dusk. The sound of Chris's skull cracking against the pavement wasn't something I could easily forget. I shuddered at the memories and continued wiping down the tables. I had recently been promoted to evening supervisor, which came with a raise and keys to lock up at night. It felt good to be treated like an adult even though I was only seventeen.

I normally closed the store on my own, and Lucas conveniently had a craving for a London Fog right before closing every time, but he wasn't there yet. I pulled out my phone and sent him a quick text.

You still coming tonight?

Lately he'd been so busy helping Nate that his absence was getting noticeable. I might need to have a talk with Nate about how much of Lucas's time he was monopolizing. I smiled, knowing full well I'd be doing no such thing. The look on Nate's face the other night flashed through my mind. He had seemed confused when Lucas had been late running his errand. Almost like... *No he wouldn't lie to me.*

My phone buzzed in my pocket.

I can't make it tonight. See you at school?

I put the phone back in my pocket and sighed. Looked like I was closing up without him.

Thankfully I had help this time; I shot a grateful look at Jenna, who was manning the cash like a pro. It felt weird but oddly empowering to be in charge of someone else for a shift. She was a couple of years younger than me. Her blue eyes had the kind of calm energy that put you at ease instantly.

There was a lull in tables needing wiped off, so I snuck a peek at my phone to see if the adoption registry had gotten back to me yet; still nothing. It had been over a week. How long did it take to run someone's name against everyone who had registered over the years?

I hadn't meant to be hopeful, but I could feel the expectation growing anyway. He had had seventeen years to simply add his name to a registry. Obviously, he would have done that. Right? I nodded to myself. He had wanted to keep me, even fought for me in court. There was no way he wouldn't have done everything possible to make sure I could find him. I wondered what he would be like. Did I look like him? Would our eyes twinkle the same way? Did he have dimples in his cheeks too?

As I continued daydreaming about the things we'd do together when we met, a man shuffled into the store. He was an older gentleman with dark skin, tattered clothing, and a frayed baseball cap he kept low on his face. He nervously toyed with a rip in his plaid shirt, and I noticed that his shoes were so worn I could practically see through them.

"May I sit down?" He spoke so softly I hardly heard him, but I smiled and beckoned him to sit at the table I'd just wiped down.

"What can I get started for you?"

He looked uncomfortable as he shifted in his seat and kept his head down.

"I don't have any money, ma'am."

"It's on the house."

I surprised myself by squeezing his arm gently. He looked up at me and his soft brown eyes glistened.

"I would love a coffee with cream and sugar." The corners of his mouth lifted slightly, and his gaze returned to the table while he wrung his hands nervously.

I went behind the counter and began preparing his coffee in the biggest mug I could find. I grabbed an assortment of treats from the display and put them on a plate. Something about him seemed so familiar to me. I took everything over and placed it on the table without a word. He nodded his thanks, and I smiled warmly as I went back behind the cash register.

"Do you know him?" Jenna's head was cocked to the side.

"I don't. I just..." I trailed off. I could hardly understand the connection myself, never mind trying to explain it to someone else. I imagined that my birth father might look something like this obviously homeless man sitting a few feet from me. Ali seemed to believe he had been headed down a dark path seventeen years ago. Maybe he had never recovered. Maybe the loss of his first-born child was too much to bear.

I watched as the homeless man nursed his coffee and nibbled on the macadamia nut cookie. My eyes welled up and I shook my head. *Snap out of it, Liv. You don't even know the guy.*

Jenna gave me a small smile and grabbed the broom to begin

the final closing tasks. I glanced at the oversized barnwood clock on the wall and was shocked to see we only had a few minutes until we closed. I hurried to the back to tidy up the office and make sure everything was ready for the morning. When I went back out front, the man was gone. I swallowed the inexplicable lump in my throat and slowly walked over to his table to clean up. He had taken the rest of the sweets, which I was happy about. Just as I was about to crumple the napkin, I noticed the words on it.

THANK YOU FOR YOUR KINDNESS.

THE LUMP GREW as I stared at the words until they blurred. I carefully folded the napkin and put it in my pocket as though it was a treasure I needed to hold on to. It was such a simple thing, giving a homeless man some coffee and food, but somehow I had a feeling the experience had just become a core memory.

IT WAS Saturday morning and I was at Le Petit Pain, a small French bakeshop that displayed art from local artists. Mixed in with the art were cartoonish paintings of loaves of bread, croissants, and pastries—almost as though they didn't want you to forget the real reason you were there. I had thrown on my comfiest sweats with an off-the-shoulder black t-shirt. My hair was in a messy bun, and I hadn't bothered with makeup, so I kept my head down as I waited to get in. It was a popular location and a line had already formed. I was near the back when I heard my name called at the front. Of course, I would run into someone I knew.

"Nate?"

I was surprised to see him there. He waved me over, much to

the annoyance of the lady behind him. I smiled apologetically as I tiptoed into line beside him. His blond hair was hidden under a white baseball cap with a logo so small I couldn't tell what it was. He was in board shorts and a light blue long sleeve shirt that matched his eyes.

"I didn't know you liked this place."

"It's not my usual go to," I admitted, "but they have the best butter tarts in the city and my parents are big fans."

"They sent you? Aren't they usually garage-saling at this time?" He tapped his watch with a playful smile.

I elbowed him in the ribs as I laughed. "Yeah, they're definitely garage-saling. I thought it'd be a nice thing to do. They've been a bit stressed lately." I was making sure that I was still on my best behavior. We moved up the line a spot and he gave me a worried look.

"Nothing too serious I hope?"

Though I wanted to confide in him, I felt myself holding back.

"Nah, I'm sure they'll bounce back. Especially after these butter tarts." After Nate laughed easily, I asked, "How are you doing? Lucas told me about you flunking science. That's gotta be hard." I sympathized with him. I hated science.

He took a bite of the licorice I hadn't noticed. "Oh, that?" He snorted. "I don't care. I want to be a musician, not a scientist. I'm just putting my time in until we graduate next year."

He stepped forward and placed his order as I stood gaping at his back. Didn't care? Lucas had been practically killing himself trying to help him pull his grade back up. If he couldn't care less, then why was Lucas working so hard? I made a mental note to ask him about it later. I placed my butter tart order and made small talk with Nate until he got the food and took off to practice his guitar riff.

Maybe I'd ask Mela about Nate. My parents weren't going to be home for at least an hour, so I made a quick decision and headed to Mela's instead of home.

Pulling up to her driveway, I was surprised to see the garden full of weeds and the grass much longer than usual. I normally just walked in, but today I hesitated. Finally, I knocked on the door and waited. Steps approached, and I took a step back as the door opened.

"Olivia?"

Mr. Moretti's eyebrows were creased in confusion. Likely because I was standing outside and hadn't just walked in. I took in his appearance and nearly did a double take. He was usually so well put together, but today he was wearing ratty sweats with what I could only conclude were food stains. His Rolling Stones t-shirt was totally frayed at the neck and looked at least twenty years old. His thick head of hair was disheveled, and his five o'clock shadow was practically a beard. I had never seen him like this.

"Hey Mr. M..." I waited for him to let me in, and it took a beat longer than it usually would.

His smile was strained as he gestured me inside. "Sorry, Olivia. Please forgive my appearance. I haven't had a chance to do the laundry this week."

He rubbed the back of his neck as I followed him into the house. My stomach was churning, but I wasn't sure why.

"Carmella!" he called from the bottom of the stairs while I found a seat in the living room.

Something was wrong, but I didn't know what. Mela came down the stairs slowly, shoulders slumped, wearing her oversized, pink and purple breakup sweater. She only wore that polka-dot sweater when she was sad about a boy. Surely, she would have told me if she and Nate had broken up. *Why is she wearing that?* Her hair looked in desperate need of a wash, or at the very least a brush-through.

"What's up, Dad?" She sounded tired. He didn't respond and instead merely pointed to where I was sitting on the couch. "Oh!" She perked up a bit when she saw me.

Her dad shuffled up the stairs and I thought I heard him

sigh. She sat in the recliner across from me and pulled her knees up to her chest.

I didn't waste any time. "What's going on, Mel?" My heart was spluttering all over the place.

"My mom is sick." It came out as a whisper. Our eyes locked, and the years of friendship between us acted like a conduit. It was bad. I could feel it.

"How sick?" I practically choked on the words. I didn't really want to know. She looked away and wrung her fingers together. I remained perfectly still as though moving even an inch would cause the news to be worse.

"We don't know yet. They're running a lot of tests right now." She saw the look on my face and added, "My mom didn't want to worry anyone unnecessarily, so she asked us not to say anything."

I nodded silently and let my breath out. Judging by Nate's lighthearted banter at the bakery, he had no idea this was going on either.

"I'm sorry, Mel. What can I do?"

She let out a shaky breath as her eyes filled with tears. I gave her a moment to compose herself.

"Just sit with me?"

Her tone transported me back to when we were six and she'd had a bad dream sleeping over. I had snuggled in beside her and held her hand until she fell back to sleep. I walked over to the recliner and squished in beside her, gripping her hand tightly. A steady stream of tears slid down her cheeks and I agonized over what magical words I could produce that might reduce the pain. I stared out the window at the clouds rolling in. In the end I stayed silent and simply held space for my longest friend, letting her tears soak my shirt. I couldn't take this away from her, but I sure as hell wasn't about to let her deal with it alone.

4

I still hadn't heard back from the adoption registry. My frustration, for the moment, was again overshadowed by the hope I hadn't meant to feel. Seventeen years was a long time to simply add your name to a registry.

But what if he hasn't? Stop it, Liv; think positive thoughts.

I nodded to myself. He'd fought for me in court, those weren't the actions of a man who had no interest in finding his daughter. Again, I wondered what he would be like. Would he be much taller than me? Would our laughs sound the same? Was he athletic too?

"Olivia!" Coach Addison's furious shout broke through my thoughts.

"Sorry, Coach," I mumbled as I forced my feet to move. I had forgotten I was even at track practice.

"Usually when the starting gun goes off"—he stormed toward me—"the runner is expected to…oh, gee, I don't know…RUN!"

He was now jogging beside me to continue yelling in my face. He whipped around and stomped back to the finish line, gesturing angrily with his arms as though talking to some imaginary sympathizer.

Between waiting to hear about Renae's test results and thinking about my birth father, I had been distracted all week. We were in final prep mode, with the upcoming track meet around the corner. I rounded the last turn and my legs felt like lead. Every step was like pulling my feet out of the mud. The entire team had lapped me, and they were now stretching on the grass while I still had a full lap to go. I slowed down to a walk as coach Addison hurled his clipboard to the ground.

"Oh, I don't think so, Olivia! You're going to finish this run if it takes you all friggin' night!"

I wiped his spittle off my cheek and picked up the pace. I focused on the faint traffic sounds coming from the highway nearby. One foot in front of the other, fists clenched, breathe in through the nose, out through the mouth. By the time I crossed the finish line for the second time, the rest of the team was packing up to leave. Coach Addison was standing in front of me with his arms folded.

"This is an embarrassment, Olivia. You're not even trying anymore, and frankly you're letting the whole team down."

I glanced over at my teammates, who were conveniently avoiding eye contact, and noticed that Lucas was sitting on the grass, having shown up somewhere between the starting gun going off and me standing still and wiping coach Addison's spittle from my cheek. *Perfect.*

"If you're going to have any shot of placing at the track meet in two weeks, then you'd better get your head in the game." He pounded his fist against the side of his head and stomped off toward the school.

I walked to my duffle bag and water bottle and picked them up carefully. Lucas approached, pulled the strap of my bag and shifted it to his shoulder, wordlessly sliding his hand into mine.

"You picked a great practice to come to," I mumbled, looking down at the ground.

He pulled me to a stop, turned my shoulders toward him and

tilted my chin up. I could feel the corners of my mouth turning down the way they did right before I cried, and I willed myself to hold it together.

"I'm sorry I haven't been to more practices lately. And honestly, Liv, your coach is a bit of a douche."

I tried to fight the smile, but I couldn't help letting it spread across my face. I studied him while he rubbed my cheek softly and noticed the purple circles under his eyes.

"Are you getting enough sleep?"

"Probably not."

Lucas smiled wryly and ran his hand through his shaggy hair. I glanced sideways at him as we walked to my car in silence. He seemed different somehow. Something wasn't adding up about all his extracurriculars for Nate. *What isn't he telling me?*

"What are you doing tonight?" He tossed my duffle bag into my back seat while I leaned against the driver's door.

"You mean other than wallowing in self-pity over how this track practice went?"

His eyes crinkled as he stifled a laugh. "Yeah, other than that."

"I could probably tear myself away for a bit. Why, what do you have in mind?"

He pressed his forehead against mine, and his sudden nearness caused my heart to skip a beat.

"It's a surprise. Be ready in an hour, I'll pick you up." He kissed my lips gently before jogging over to his truck. "I can feel you watching me, you know!" he called out playfully, and I shook my head with a smirk.

At home I took my time showering off the layer of disapproval Coach Addison had left me with. I thought about what Lucas could be hiding from me, but nothing made sense. Then I used the cucumber melon shampoo because it was his favorite. The scent seemed to wake me up and help me decide to just trust that Lucas would tell me what was going on when he was ready.

He hadn't pressed me to talk when I nearly drowned myself in the ocean after meeting Ali. I could afford him some time.

I was in a considerably better mood after my shower and chose to stray from the norm and put on an emerald dress with spaghetti straps and a light jacket just in case it got chilly, though that was unlikely during May in Florida. I straightened my hair and curled the ends, then put on some makeup. I wasn't sure what he was planning, but I would be ready.

My parents were having tea in the living room when I came upstairs. The television was on, but they weren't watching it.

"I'm heading out, guys."

My mom jumped a little at my words and my dad didn't seem to realize that I had even been home.

"Where you going, kiddo?"

I smiled at my dad's endearing nickname for me. "Out with Lucas. I'll be home by curfew," I threw in before my mom could remind me.

She smiled without looking over, and I stepped out the door to wait outside. I still had a few minutes before Lucas picked me up, so I sent Mela a text checking in for the millionth time. She wrote back pretty quickly.

> I'm still as okay as I was three hours ago. I both love and hate you for being such an annoyingly awesome best friend. Oh, and I told Nate, so you can tell Lucas if you want.

I NODDED to myself as I automatically pulled up Ali and Leah's social media feeds to scroll through them. More pictures of Ali with her daughters; on Leah's feed, she was playing in the ocean waves with pure joy on her face. I couldn't help but smile as I zoomed in. We had the same nose.

My phone dinged again, and I expected it to be another text, but to my surprise it was an email with the subject "Adoption Registry Results for Olivia Jackson." My heart flew into my throat. I didn't have a chance to read it before Lucas's truck threw its lights on my steps. I tossed my phone into my purse, stood up and walked over to his truck. If it was bad news, I didn't want it to ruin our night. It would still be there later.

Lucas had hopped out of the truck and walked around to open my door for me. His hazel-green eyes popped as he took in my appearance. I felt myself blush.

"W-wow."

He cleared his throat as his voice caught. I could have said the same thing. He was in khaki shorts and a thin white short-sleeve shirt that emphasized the definition of his arms. His hair was ruffled and slightly damp from his shower. I smiled and tried to move past, but his hand on my stomach made my breath catch. I looked up at him questioningly.

"Liv, I haven't been the best boyfriend lately. I've missed too many of your track practices, I haven't been around enough after your shifts... This is my apology date."

He leaned down and kissed my cheek, then helped me up into the truck. I blinked back the threatening tears as we pulled out of my driveway.

"Where are we going anyway?" I looked out the window at the sky. The sun was just beginning to set.

"You'll see." He smiled as I pretended to pout at his secrecy.

A few minutes later he drove right onto a very secluded part of the beach and positioned the truck so that the back was closest to the water. I hopped out as he reached into the back seat for supplies I hadn't noticed before. Gently he pushed my hand away when I tried to help, so I turned and walked toward the water, enjoying the feel of the setting sun on my face. It was my favorite kind of sunset when the puffy clouds changed colors. It was still too early for that, but I knew it was coming. The sun was making a perfect golden triangle on the top of the water sparkling its way toward me.

After a few minutes, Lucas called me back over to him. My eyes widened as I took in the scene. The bottom and sides of the truck bed were covered in blankets, while pillows lined the back. A string of twinkling lights wrapped around the whole truck bed, and snacks were laid out on a serving tray I recognized from Nate's place.

"Wow, Lucas," I whispered.

Smiling, he reached out to pull me up into the truck. Flashbacks of the many moments when he had done the same thing brought a smile to my face. I reached up to let him pull me and noticed right away that the truck bed was much softer than I had anticipated. I bent down and realized there was a thin inflatable mattress below the blankets. He had truly thought of everything.

I sat and made myself comfy while he slid in beside me. Our arms touched as we munched on crackers, cheese and strawberries and watched the colors of the clouds transform from golden to wisps of cotton candy before our eyes. We sat in silence, needing no words to convey the comfort between us.

"Have you heard back from the adoption registry yet? It's been a while," he finally asked.

I could hear the hesitation in his voice, and I sighed.

"I actually just got an email back from them right before you picked me up." I held up my hand before he could say what he was about to. "I haven't opened it yet. I didn't want to ruin our night if it was bad news."

My chest tightened as I watched the horizon turn a beautiful shade of orange. He seemed to be processing my words as he sat much stiller than usual beside me.

"You don't want to open it with me?" He sounded hurt. *Crap.*

"No, no, Lucas—it's not that I don't want to share the news with you—of course I do—but if it's bad, I'm going to be all depressed and…" I trailed off.

"You didn't want me to see that?" he mumbled quietly, and

after a minute added almost as an afterthought, "You can trust me with the hard stuff too. You know that."

I did know that, but I was tired of him seeing the hard stuff. It felt like the entire duration of our relationship had been slanted toward the bad stuff up until now. It was time for some happy news. Wasn't it? I sighed again.

"I wanted tonight to be about just us. It feels like we've hardly spent time together lately." The sky was now a beautiful violet color, and the sun was long gone.

"That's fair. I'm here if you do want to open it tonight, though."

He put his arm around my shoulder and pulled me closer. I wrapped my arm around his waist and rested my head on his chest, listening to the steady drum of his heart.

"Mela's mom is sick," I whispered into his chest. I felt him stiffen, and his arm squeezed my shoulder.

"How sick?" His voice was tight.

"I'm not sure yet. They're still doing testing, but I can tell that Mela and her dad are really worried."

"How are you doing with it?"

"I'm not totally sure. I mean, she's my second mom, ya know? But until I have all the facts, there isn't much sense in freaking out." It sounded *adulty.*

"But you're still freaking out?" I could hear the small smile behind his words.

"Yep."

The "p" popped a little harder than I meant it to. There was really no fooling Lucas. He knew me way too well. It was both incredibly special and very unnerving. I wanted to change the subject, so I asked about his dad. The last I had heard, his mom had sent his dad away when he came looking, and we hadn't really talked about it too much since then. Anytime I brought it up, he shut down a little. He was helping me with the search for my dad, though, so I felt it was only fair that I ask about his.

"He's a ghost. I haven't been able to find out anything about where he might be. But maybe that's for the best." I felt his jaw tighten as it rested on my head.

"You can't give up. He's out there and he came looking for you. That means something." My resolve was building. He couldn't give up because of a few dead ends. I wouldn't let him.

"You sound like me," he whispered the words into my ear, causing my shoulder to rise as tingles shot down my arm.

I needed a moment to regain my composure. "I guess you're rubbing off on me."

The now indigo sky made me smile. It had been such a beautiful sunset, and the first stars were beginning to make an appearance. I shivered a little and Lucas immediately reached over and wrapped a blanket around me. As I listened to the waves gently crashing onto the sand, I traced my fingers absentmindedly across his chest.

"Do you remember what you said to me that night about me maybe being the one to save my birth dad?"

"Sort of." His fingers were dancing up and down my arm and it was getting harder to concentrate.

"I've thought about that a lot. It's the hope I've held on to all these months. So, uh, thanks."

My voice was thick with emotion. I wondered if he knew how often his words had replayed in my mind over the last many months. Our eyes locked, and understanding passed between us. He gently pressed his lips against mine and I melted into him. My heart felt like it had exploded as shivers shot up the length of my spine. His lips slowly parted mine, and he tasted incredible. My hands moved into his hair as I pulled his neck closer to me.

What was once a soft and slow kiss had increased in intensity. I leaned back and pulled him down with me so that he was half on top of me as our lips remained locked together. One of his arms supported his weight so that he wouldn't crush me while he ran his fingers through my hair. My hands were everywhere—in his hair, on his neck, pulling his body closer to mine.

He was kissing my lips, my neck, my collarbone, my lips again; it was intoxicating. I slid my hand up his shirt and ran it along his abs as he groaned and seemed to struggle with himself. He sighed and reluctantly stopped, rolling away from me. We were both breathing heavily as he placed his arm over his eyes.

"Sorry, Liv."

His eyes were still closed. I stayed silent as my heart regained its normal rhythm. A shooting star streaked across the sky, and I listened to the sounds of the ocean until my racing pulse had steadied. He looked over at me sheepishly and I smirked back at him. We weren't really all that sorry, and one of these days we wouldn't stop ourselves, when the time was right.

LATER THAT NIGHT I found myself under the covers in bed staring at the words on my phone in disbelief.

DEAR MS. JACKSON,

We received your request to match you with any potential biological family members. Unfortunately, no one has requested to be matched with you at this time. We will keep your request on file for six months, after which time your account will go inactive.

Sincerely,

The National Adoption Registry

THE SUDDEN KNOT in my stomach was preventing me from taking a deep breath. The sounds coming out of my chest were raspy and quick. *He doesn't want to be found.* The words stung as tears burned behind my eyelids, threatening to spill over. I squeezed my eyes as tightly as I could until I saw stars, then slowly let out my breath.

At least I didn't open this in front of Lucas. It would have been so much worse to have read that in front of anyone. Rejection was humiliating enough without an audience. I shrugged and took shaky breath after shaky breath until I felt steady. *Oh, well, better to know now than having wasted more time looking for someone who doesn't want to be found.*

The thought brought very little comfort, but I knew if I rehearsed it enough, I'd eventually believe it myself. I hoped so anyway. I'd believed things were looking up, but I was wrong. Dead wrong.

5

Things went from bad to worse. The track meet had been an absolute disaster. Not only had I not placed in any of the events, but I also didn't come anywhere near my personal best times. I was getting worse, and Coach Addison was so furious that he suspended me from the team until my head "was on straight again."

Lucas didn't even show up to the meet. That night had been so perfect and he had said all the right things, but I couldn't ignore his absence anymore. It had been weeks of secrecy—I was done. There was one person other than Lucas who knew what was going on, and I needed answers.

I pulled up to Nate's house and parked on the street instead of the driveway.

I'm outside, we need to talk. DON'T tell Lucas.

I COULD SEE the gray bubble with dots and knew he was responding.

. . .

Okay...

I PACED BACK and forth in front of my car while I waited for him to come out. It was a warm, breezy Sunday afternoon and I turned my gaze up to the sun while my hair flew around my face. I was suddenly grateful that Nate's driveway was so long and that thick bushes lined the front of his house so I was hidden from view. He came around the corner wearing pyjama pants and a Radiohead t-shirt, rubbing his eyes like he had just woken up.

"What's going on, Liv?"

His blue eyes were full of concern, and I nearly wavered in my decision to put him in this predicament, but I had to know what Lucas was hiding.

"I could ask you the same thing, Nate."

There was an edge to my voice I hadn't intended. His eyes widened at my tone, and he ran his hand through his messy hair.

"Liv..." His own tone held a warning.

"You know what he's hiding, Nate. He's been disappearing for weeks, and I know he hasn't been helping you get your *grades* back up."

"I can't tell you, Liv. I'm sorry."

He did look sorry, but he hadn't even hesitated before shutting me down. His eyes kept darting from his house and to me. I wasn't sure if he had told Lucas that I was there or not, but I had the feeling that he'd be coming out soon if I didn't hurry this conversation along.

"We've been friends for years, Nate. That doesn't count for anything, I guess?" I was hitting him where it hurt, and I knew it.

"You know it counts, Liv. But I can't betray my best friend

like that. He's *not* cheating on you. I can tell you that much at least."

His eyes now begged me to believe him, and I took a deep breath as I turned away. I could let it go—*but how many more things am I going to have to just accept in my life?*

"It's not good enough, Nate. We both know it." I got back into my car, and he didn't try to stop me as I drove away.

I WHIPPED another rock at the baseball diamond by my house and smiled with satisfaction at the way it hit the ground, causing an explosion of rocks to fly. *Bullseye.* The dark clouds in the distance foreshadowed the impending storm. There was a chill in the air and I should feel cold, but instead I was numb. I kind of liked the emptiness, and that knowledge was unsettling.

I reached down to pick up another rock just as the rain began. It was not a gentle sprinkle, and I was drenched in less than a minute. I pitched rock after rock until I ran out of strength. I was done. I was going to quit the team and I was damn well not going to look for my birth father anymore. *There, that settles it.*

It didn't feel settled, not by a long shot, but I was done thinking about it. I turned around to leave and caught sight of Lucas heading my way. I immediately headed in the opposite direction.

"Liv!"

I could barely hear him over the rain, and I continued walking. Suddenly he was gently grabbing my arm and turning me around to face him.

"Would you just stop?" He sounded impatient.

I looked down at his hand icily until he dropped my arm.

"You came to see Nate but not me?" he said.

I looked at him, trying to decipher how much of our conversation Nate had relayed.

"I had some questions for him."

"Yeah, he told me. Look I'm sorry I haven't been around…" He trailed off as though expecting me to interrupt him; I didn't.

"Where *have* you been?" I wasn't beating around the bush anymore.

"I'm sorry." His eyes were downcast, but he didn't offer more.

"Sorry but you're still not going to tell me?" I demanded, my hands now on my hips. "How am I supposed to trust you?" I could feel the tears fighting to escape.

"You just are. Haven't we been through enough together for you to believe that I wouldn't do anything to hurt you?"

He grabbed my hand as his eyes bore into mine. I jutted out my chin and pulled my hand away from his.

"I guess not."

He ran his hands through his wet hair and grabbed fists of it before dropping his hands and clenching his jaw.

"I'm not ready to tell you about this part of my life." He said it with finality.

"That's fine, Lucas. I'll just add you to the list of guys I can't rely on." My voice cracked on the last word, and I cleared my throat quickly.

He took a step back with his arms up in defense. "Liv, that's not fair—" He broke off mid-sentence, and his face suddenly registered understanding. "You read the email." It wasn't a question.

I glared at him as I turned away, letting the icy drops of rain mask the tears that had just slid down my cheeks.

"It doesn't matter," I muttered. "I'm done searching for someone who doesn't want to be found."

"Why didn't you tell me he didn't register? I didn't even know you'd read the email."

"I would have if you'd been around," I threw back at him.

"I have been around. There were plenty of opportunities to tell me and you know it." His voice was strained.

I simply shrugged with my back still turned.

"So, you're just done then?" he insisted.

I stayed silent staring off into the woods while rain continued to pelt my face.

"Liv, come *on*. He didn't register and that sucks but—why do you do this?"

His voice had dropped to barely above a whisper and I had to strain to hear him. I turned to face him, and my eyes flashed up at his, but I said nothing. The rain dripped off his hair and down his cheeks, resembling tears. He went on.

"Why do you give up so easily when things get hard?"

"Excuse me?" He didn't seem to know what he was getting himself into.

"You do, Liv, and you know it. You fight for others so damn hard, but when it comes to you..." He trailed off, seemed to gather himself and continued. "Last year you braved your psychotic ex just to make sure I didn't end up in jail, but now you hit a simple setback with your dad, and you're just done?"

I recoiled at the sting of his words. A simple *setback*? Sure, it was just one registry, and maybe he had looked in some other capacity—but what if he hadn't? I knew how much *this* hurt and I couldn't risk going any further.

"First of all, he's not my *dad*. At this point he's just an idea. An idea I'm not sure I want to pursue anymore."

"Liv—"

"You don't get to decide this for me!"

It was the first time I had ever raised my voice at him. He flinched as though I had slapped his face. We stood apart, facing off for what felt like an eternity. Neither of us willing to give the other what they wanted. His jaw was clenched as he stared at me in disbelief. He shifted from one foot to the other and kept opening his mouth as though to say something and then he nodded—more to himself than anything—turned on his heels and left. I started after him automatically but stopped myself. Instead, I watched as he made his way through the gravel toward his truck, backed out of his parking spot and sped away.

There was an ache so deep in my chest that I pushed my fist into my side just to distract me. What could he be hiding that was so bad he'd rather walk away than tell me? I'd been practically naked emotionally and he was clammed up. I let out the breath I hadn't realized I was holding, picked up a handful of gravel and hurled it at the fence. I could do this alone. I didn't need track, my birth father, or Lucas. *I've survived worse than this.* I reassured myself.

Lucas just didn't understand, and I wasn't about to count on him. At the end of the day, I was the only one I could really rely on.

I started shivering involuntarily from the rain that was still pelting me. My legs felt like lead as I trudged through the wet gravel and began my walk home. The street was deserted, which just highlighted how alone I really was.

Get used to it, kiddo.

I was beginning to resent the voice inside my head.

6

"*You fight for others so damn hard but when it comes to you…*"

As much as I tried to fight it, Lucas's words continued to replay in my mind. *Dammit.* I didn't want to be a quitter. It was not like he'd know one way or the other; we hadn't spoken since our fight. I glared at the screen of the library computer, willing it to tell me what to do like a Magic 8 Ball.

Finally, I opened my email and clicked on the "only draft" tab. The hole in the sleeve of my pink shirt was like a magnet to my fingers, which could not stop burrowing in it. I stared at the cursor blinking on the half-written email I wasn't convinced I should send.

Dear Ali,

I promised myself I would never reach out to you for anything, but I need information only you can give me.

She wasn't going to help me, so why was I wasting my time?

But what was the worst that could happen? That she didn't write back?

Armed with that new belief I began typing again.

I need to know everything you can tell me about my biological father. I won't share anything about you or your family with him as you had mentioned before that you were afraid of him. If I find him, that is. But that's what I feel I need to do—find him. And you are the best chance I have of that, so I hope that you'll consider my request.

Olivia

I couldn't bring myself to hit send, so I saved it to draft. *Why does it always feel like I'm asking for her permission to exist?* I sighed loudly and got a few looks from around the library. I smiled sheepishly and closed my laptop while shoving the rest of my things in my bag. *I need some air.*

Once in my car, I began heading toward Mela's automatically, then winced.

You fight for others so damn hard... Except for this. I hadn't been fighting "so hard" for my best friend. "I'm fine, everything will be fine," she had said with a look that conveyed we were done discussing it.

The tests had come back, and the news about Renae wasn't good—stage four pancreatic cancer. The doctors were treating it aggressively, but it would be a race against time. I didn't know how to support Mela. I wanted to, desperately. But I had never even lost a pet before. How was I supposed to support someone who might be losing her mom?

I saw the familiar turn to her street and found myself driving right by it. Instead, before I knew it, I was pulling up to a familiar apartment complex, parking in the last visitor's spot, and letting myself into Adam and Isabel's lobby. We had become close after spending Thanksgiving together last year. Their building was rundown, with cracks in the yellowed paint, water-stained ceilings, and flickering fluorescent lights along the hallway. There was no elevator, so I took the stairs to their second-floor apartment.

I hesitated outside the door before knocking. What if their

daughter was sleeping? I listened for a couple of seconds and heard Nori squeal. I smiled as I knocked on the door and waited. Adam opened the door holding Nori on his hip like any experienced parent. His blond, curly hair was disheveled, and his boyish features had faded slightly as his face matured and the lack of sleep made him look older than he was. Still handsome, just tired.

"Liv, hey!" I had surprised him.

"Hey..." I looked into the apartment but didn't see Isabel.

"She's at work."

He stepped aside to make room for me to come in and I scooped Nori into my arms and blew a raspberry on her stomach, which made her shriek with laughter. I puffed out my cheeks and crossed my eyes as she grinned and grabbed fistfuls of my hair. Adam rushed to untangle my hair from her death grip as I grimaced with pain.

"I'm sorry, I should have called first." I sat down on their orange velvet couch, the only furniture in their living room aside from a very old bean bag chair and snuggled Nori into the crook of my arm.

"You know you're always welcome." He threw me a grateful glance as he tidied up the toys on the floor.

I played peekaboo with Nori and smiled as her brown eyes crinkled and her curly dark hair bounced up and down with each excited arm flap. I kissed the top of her head and breathed in deeply, drawing comfort from the new baby smell. She smelled like warm summer skin and fresh clean cotton. She smelled like life.

"What's up, Liv?" He plopped down on the bean bag chair and gave me a knowing look. His shoulders sagged as though the weight of the world were on them.

"How are you guys doing?" I asked gently.

He closed his eyes and sank lower into the bean bag. "We're getting by. We got approved for that daycare subsidy, so we'll actually be able to afford it now. I'll pick up a few more shifts at the restaurant and Iz can switch to full time. Then we can hopefully move into a bigger place."

Nori started fussing in my arms and Adam got up to make a bottle.

"I'm really happy for you. She's lucky to have you," I murmured thoughtfully.

He was so good to Isabel. He didn't have to stay and take care of Nori. She wasn't technically his daughter, after all. As I watched him cradle her into his arm and pop the bottle in her mouth with the familiarity of a father, I realized that I was wrong. He was in this. Nori was his daughter, as far as he was concerned. I strongly suspected he and Isabel were more than friends at this point, but they weren't ready to admit it, so I left it alone.

"We're a family. Not exactly traditional, but it works." He shrugged easily as Nori finished the bottle with her eyelids drooping.

"That it does." I stood up and moved toward the door. He had his hands full.

"Why did you stop by, Liv?" He was swaying Nori back and forth, and I was mesmerized by the peaceful look on her chubby little face.

"Just needed some girl chat. Sorry, but you don't qualify—and she's not quite old enough yet." I smirked as he clutched his chest, feigning insult.

"Trouble in paradise?" He waggled his eyebrows at me as Nori snored softly in his arms.

"Something like that."

My eyes blurred for a moment, and I waved softly as I snuck out while he put his daughter down for her nap. I rested the back of my head against the closed door for a moment before gathering the strength I needed to leave.

I had been sitting in my room for so long that the only light came from my laptop. I was reading and re-reading the draft email debating on whether I should send it or not. Both my parents were working late tonight, so I was on my own with my frustrations. The last thing I wanted to do was admit that I needed Ali's help, but I was at a dead end. It was either this, or I gave up entirely. As Lucas had so lovingly pointed out, I had a habit of giving up, and I didn't want that to be true. I looked out at the indigo sky and noticed the napkin pinned to my cork board.

Thank you for your kindness.

The homeless man at Brew was so soft-spoken and gentle, but his eyes were haunted. If I could somehow find my birth father, I knew that I'd be able to help him. Homelessness or prison wouldn't have to be his story. Maybe I'd been feeling so out of sync because I needed to know him. Maybe he had a good reason for not including his name on the adoption registry.

I pressed send. It was out of my hands now. All I could do was wait and see.

7

It turns out I didn't have to wait long for Ali's response. I found it in my inbox the next morning when I finally rolled over to check my phone. I bit my lip as I cautiously tapped on the unread email.

Olivia,

I cannot divulge the information that you have requested. As I told you when we met, I'm sure he was on his way to prison or worse. Even if he got his life together, which I doubt, have you considered that you may be invading his privacy if he has reasons for not wanting to be found? Maybe you should reconsider this course of action.

Ali

My fists were clenched so tightly that my nails were digging into my palms. *How dare she?* I wanted to be angry, and I was. But a bigger part of me knew that her words held a truth I had been burying beneath the surface of my hope. *Maybe he doesn't want to be found.* It had been there all along, but seeing the words on the screen was like a slap in the face.

I quickly brushed away the tears sliding down my cheeks and began pacing my bedroom floor. *Why should I have to ask for permission to know who my biological father is?* In no time the beige wall-to-wall carpet had begun to look worn where I had been walking back and forth. *How is this not against my human rights?* Most people on the planet knew who both their parents were. It was right there on their birth certificate, for crying out loud.

I started as if lightning had struck. *My birth certificate! Of course!* I immediately flung my door open and ran up the stairs. Why hadn't I thought of that before? It seemed so obvious. I forced myself to saunter into the kitchen instead of storming in the way I wanted to.

"Hey Mom…" I walked over casually and stood by the stove as she stirred a giant pot of spaghetti sauce—vegetarian, of course. Her monthly tradition to fill the deep freeze with re-usable containers full of ready-made food.

"Hey, honey, can you pass the oregano?" she asked absent-mindedly as she squinted over a heavily stained recipe card.

Silently I passed the spice jar as I mustered the courage to ask for my birth certificate. The smell of oregano, garlic, and tomato filled the air. Her familiar apron was tied around her thin frame, its ruffled white straps frayed from years of use. She seemed to notice me standing there for the first time and gave me a quizzical look.

"You okay, honey?" Her tone was hesitant, as though saying, "I'll be there for you if you need me, but I also kind of hope you don't."

You may be overthinking this, I chided myself.

"Oh, yeah, I'm fine, Mom." I shot her a quick smile and grabbed a glass of water. I sipped it slowly and began to lose my nerve as I started to walk out of the kitchen. Just as I was halfway out, I forced myself to turn, and I snapped my fingers above my head as though I had just remembered something.

"Hey, can I see my birth certificate?"

Her eyebrows creased together, and I braced myself for her answer. "It's upstairs in the cedar chest."

My heart sank. The cedar chest was an old dark chest six feet long, two feet wide, and about three feet high. I nearly fell in once as a kid trying to snoop. It contained all the gifts, jewelry, and items that were most special to my mom and, most importantly, it was off limits. There was no way she was going to let me in there.

She gave me a sideways look and I could see that she was about to say no.

"It's for my doctor's appointment, to keep me qualified for the track team." I blurted it out much too quickly and held my breath. I felt guilty at the lie but knew it was for the best. I still hadn't told my parents that I was looking for my birth father, and they really didn't need anything added to their plates right now.

"I suppose so since it's for the doctor. Top right side in an envelope labelled 'Olivia.'"

I smiled and offered my thanks, then flew up the stairs to her sewing room. The chest was at the very front of the room, as always, and I eagerly pulled the chest open and held the lid high above my head as I searched for the envelope. I couldn't help but look around a little. There was a heart-shaped jewelry box I had never seen before containing a diamond-studded bracelet. There were several journals that looked worn from use. As I flipped through, I saw that they were in my mother's handwriting. There was a box with four pairs of baby shoes that I assumed were mine and my siblings'. I didn't waste too much time looking through everything. The pull to find a name on my birth certificate was stronger than the pull to snoop.

My pulse quickened when I saw it. It was a large white envelope resting on top of an old blue sweater I used to wear religiously. The white had faded to yellow over the years and the envelope felt delicate between my fingers, and lighter than I had expected. I let the lid of the chest close slowly and set it back down without a sound, as though what I was about to do required a hushed silence. I tiptoed over to my mother's vintage sewing table—vintage because it was a good deal at a garage sale—and sat on the surprisingly comfortable mesh-backed roller chair. I carefully pushed aside some fabric to make room for the envelope, took a deep breath and unraveled the nylon string holding it closed.

Sliding my hand inside the envelope, I pulled out a thin stack of papers. On the very top was the record of my adoption. I read through it carefully, but it only contained what I had already seen before. My birth name was listed as Rose Schafer, which was Ali's maiden name, but it didn't help identify my birth father. I moved the adoption record to the left and a smaller piece of paper fell off the table. My heart leapt into my throat as I realized what it was. With trembling hands, I picked up my birth certificate and hungrily looked for where my biological parents were listed. My stomach clenched as my eyes fell upon the blank space where my birth father's name should have been. The paper seemed to be trembling, but I realized it was simply my eyes moving side to side so quickly that it was making the page blurry. I shifted my jaw back and forth.

"How was she allowed to leave his name off of my birth certificate?" I demanded aloud. I tossed it carelessly on top of my adoption record and looked through the rest of the paperwork. There was a second birth certificate with my name typed as Olivia Jackson and my adoptive parents' names listed on it instead of Ali's. I suddenly realized that having access to my original birth certificate probably wasn't a luxury all adoptees had. I hadn't known that our history could be legally wiped out that way. It left a bad taste in my mouth.

To my surprise, hidden with the rest of the contents was a letter I didn't recognize.

To Whom It May Concern:

My name is (REDACTED) and I am the father of Rose

Schafer. Although I would very much like to keep her, I have been persuaded that she would be better off being raised by two parents. I still have a lot of growing up to do and it would be in her best interest for me to terminate my parental rights.

Sincerely,

(REDACTED)

My breath caught in my throat as I read and reread the letter a dozen times. I held it to the light, even though I knew it was a futile gesture. His name was right there; only, it wasn't. Though these papers had always been available to me, I had believed it best not to pry. I didn't want to rock the boat. I didn't want to seem ungrateful for the life my parents had sacrificed so much to give me. My parents had made sure that I had always had the connection to Ali, and they were very forthcoming. It would have been selfish to push for more. I didn't want them to think that I resented being adopted. Even if a part of me did feel that way.

I read it again. The word *persuaded* practically jumped off the page each time I saw it. *Persuaded.* My nostrils flared. My father had wanted me, fought for me, took Ali to court for me. Someone had gone to great lengths to make sure that he gave up. To make sure that he believed that I would be better off with two parents instead of just him.

How dare they make that decision? How dare they convince a father that his daughter would be better off without him? How dare they withhold my history, my culture, my family from me? I stared at the word *persuaded* until I was sure the letter would catch fire if I didn't look away. I thought of Ali, so flippant in her response. She would do anything to keep his name a secret—even redact it. *What the hell is she so afraid of?*

My stomach was beginning to hurt from the tension. I shouldn't have to play detective to discover where I came from. I shouldn't have to beg for scraps of information about my own life.

I could hear the tapping of my mom's slippers on the floor as she bustled in the kitchen. I ran my fingers over my birth father's handwriting, though I knew this was just a copy and not the original, redacted as it was. I leaned back and let myself be supported by the mesh on the back of the chair. My eyes floated over the different patterns of fabric strewn over the table. There were a lot of multicolored plaid and gingham pieces with a few solid colors here and there. I guessed my mom was making pillowcases again.

One more look at the letter and I snapped a quick picture of it with my phone, and then carefully placed everything inside the envelope and re-wound the nylon string around the button to seal it up. I dropped it back on top of the jewelry box and trinkets, closed the chest lid, took one last look around the room, and gently closed the door.

In the kitchen my mom was still putzing around, finishing up the dishes and waiting for her pot of tea to steep.

"Did you find what you needed?" She sounded distracted.

Turns out I was immaculately conceived, so that's cool, I guess. I snorted under my breath. "Yes," I replied simply.

I turned to leave, but there was a question burning within that I couldn't ignore.

"Mom...do you know why my birth father's letter has his name removed?" I sounded like I had a frog in my throat, and I hoped she wouldn't notice. She glanced over and sighed.

"I believe Ali's mother had the record altered before sending it to me." She wiped her hands on her apron and watched for my reaction with a pained expression before going on. "I had requested it so that you would have as much information about your past as possible, but she and Ali were adamant about you not knowing who he was. I'm sorry, honey." Her eyes were so full of pity that I had to look away; it was only making me angrier.

Poor Liv, no link to her past, no idea where she comes from. Just a second-class citizen who has to ask for her papers. I forced a smile.

"Liv..." She took a step toward me with her arm outstretched, the way she had a million times before. The smell of burning assaulted my nostrils and filled me with relief.

"The sauce is burning, Mom."

"Oh, shoot!" She whipped back around and began furiously stirring it while muttering to herself.

I escaped to my room, and there I reread Ali's email. The blood pounded in my ears and heat burned in my chest as I absorbed the dismissive tone of her words once more. My phone dinged with a notification from Instagram and the sound connected the dots in my mind. The Fourth of July was less than a week away. I mentally calculated what I would need to do to make it happen as I pulled up Ali's feed. I tapped triumphantly on the image I had seen a few days ago. It was a picture of her and her family smiling for the camera, and the caption read,

Can't wait for our annual 4th of July party at our vacation home in Boca Raton!

Boca Raton was less than a half hour away from my place. She might be able to dismiss me through email, but what would she do when we were face to face? One way or another, she was going to give me the information I was entitled to. I limbered up my shoulders and cracked my neck.

"See you soon, Ali."

8

I parked on the street several blocks from their house and walked over. It hadn't been too hard to find since I had Ali's last name and phone number. My parents thought I was working, and work thought I was sick. I felt guilty calling in on a holiday, but this was my only shot.

The area was posh but not gated-community posh, thankfully. It wasn't hard to tell which house was hosting the party. A constant stream of well-dressed middle-aged couples looking rather festive continued to arrive with gift bags of alcohol. I was starting to wonder if Ali had a liquor license for all the booze entering the premises. I looked down at my capris and white tank top and realized that I was severely underdressed. I shrugged and scoped out her place from a side street nearby.

The house was large and backed onto the beach. The interlock walkway was illuminated by decorative lanterns and lined with manicured shrubs on either side. Trellises covered in bright flowers carefully leaned up against the siding. A breeze ruffled the palm tree leaves on the property, and classy music drifted from the back patio. This wasn't your average Fourth of July barbecue.

As I walked up to the large double doors, I gave way to the

bad habit of chewing the inside of my cheek. Just as I was about to knock, the door swung open, and a curvy blonde woman stepped through backwards as she carried on a conversation she was still having.

"You are terrible, Hank! Terrible!" Her laugh indicated that she had in fact not found whatever Hank had said terrible.

She was still laughing and nearly bumped me off the walkway before turning abruptly and realizing I was there.

"Oh! I'm so sorry. Let me get out of your way. Go ahead in." She stumbled a little and lit a cigarette halfway down the driveway as Hank followed.

I turned to the open door and heard the sounds of laughter, friends greeting each other, glasses clinking and violins playing. Deciding it was as good an invitation as I was going to get, I stepped through the doorway into a brightly lit foyer packed with partygoers. This was clearly a popular event. I inhaled deeply through my nose and exhaled slowly through my mouth as I peered from side to side looking for Ali. I began walking through the house, stopping only to stare at the family pictures on the wall. There were several of Ali and her husband and daughters, all in matching attire and smiling stiffly for the camera, but some pictures appeared to be of her daughters with grandparents and even great-grandparents. Maybe mine? I wasn't sure.

A couple of waiters moved through the party, carrying trays of appetizers and champagne glasses. Twinkling lights flickered throughout a vast room. I wandered over to a large potted cactus, absentmindedly taking in its bright orange color and wondering if someone had dyed it. My hand reached for it automatically, and the sharp barbs stabbed my finger.

Wake up, Liv. I shook my head and let my hand drop away. A quick glance around reassured me that no one had noticed me, and I breathed a sigh of relief. I looked back at the door. *Maybe I should just go.*

The longer I stayed, the less confident I felt. The air began to seem thick, and my throat was constricting. *This was a mistake.* Refusing to chicken out just yet, I squeezed past groups of guests and headed to the backyard. Once outside, I greedily drank in the fresh air. In through the nose, out through the mouth. Strings of lights hung on the veranda, casting a glow throughout the yard. Small American flags were placed here and there in a "We're proud to be American" but "We're not tacky" way. The music was softer out here, and I could hear the waves crashing in the distance. My heart calmed, in tune with the waves. Groups mulled around, some sitting on furniture, others standing and having murmured conversations.

A familiar head tilted to my left and froze as I locked eyes with Ali, who was about fifteen feet away. *Well, crap. Guess I can't sneak out now.* My cheeks burned and I dropped my gaze as I clamped my teeth together to keep them from chattering. Out of my peripheral vision I watched her excuse herself from the guests she was talking to and head directly towards me. Every step somehow seemed both too fast and too slow.

She was in a sleek knee-length black dress, and her hair fell in loose curls to her shoulders. I trembled as she came closer but stood my ground. Just as she was about to pass by me, she leaned in and cupped my elbow firmly, turning me around.

"Come with me." Her voice was like ice, and just loud enough for me to hear. She smiled to each guest we passed as I followed closely, now officially freaking out and kicking myself for not having had some kind of speech prepared.

"Just a friend of the family," she'd answer to the questioning looks she received as I trailed her.

She led me down a darkened hall that was obviously not meant for guests and I waited as she unlocked a door. I glanced down the hall before following her into what looked like an office and saw a girl wearing jeans and an American-flag tank top standing there with a quizzical look on her face. I recognized Leah immediately but was too stunned to react. As soon as Ali closed the door behind us and flicked on the lights, she spoke.

"What are you doing here, Olivia?" I wasn't sure what I was expecting, but the cold calm tone of her voice wasn't it.

I cleared my throat. "I-I need you to tell me what you know about my birth father." I hated the way my voice quivered.

Her eyebrows shot up. "And you thought the best place to do that would be at a party in my home?" Her crossed arms mirrored mine.

"Well, I figured you wouldn't be able to blow me off at least."

"You're trespassing on private property."

My heart stopped. I hadn't thought of that. Would she call the police? Her icy gaze seemed to soften just a touch as she sighed.

"What is it you're hoping to find, Olivia?"

"My birth father?" It came out as a question.

She waved her hand dismissively. "Yes, obviously, but what do you hope to achieve? I gave you the answers you were looking for when we met last year."

I snorted and she cocked her head to the side in response. *This is going well.*

"I think we may remember things differently," I muttered.

"Olivia, you're not going to find what you're looking for. Not in him. He won't offer you anything new, and like I wrote in my email, he likely doesn't want to be found." She brushed off an imaginary piece of lint from her top as she sighed again. "I think you should leave."

I flinched and let out a forceful breath. "You've had a vacation home half an hour from me for years and never bothered to meet me? You're supposed to be my mother." I whispered the last part.

"I told you: I lost the right to be your mother the moment I gave you up for adoption." She turned away as she spoke.

"No one took that from you. You threw it away." *Like me.* I choked back a sob just as the door opened and interrupted whatever she was about to say in response.

"...so noisy, I just needed a little quiet."

An elderly lady in a wheelchair came into the room, pushed by Leah. I backed away instinctively. The lady in the wheelchair had a full head of white hair and green eyes that were locked on mine. I looked from her to Leah to Ali and back to her as I realized everyone in the room had identical eyes.

"Alison, dear, who's your guest?" Her voice sweet but mixed with a this-isn't-really-a-question tone.

"Sorry, G.G., Olivia was just leaving." Her voice had a finality to it that made me shudder. *I guess we're done here.*

"Yes, I apologize for the intrusion. I'll be leaving now." I shuffled to the door.

"Alison, you're being rude to your guest."

The white-haired granny had gently grabbed hold of my wrist as I tried to walk past.

"Granny, she really should be going." Ali wasn't having it, and the niceties were wearing thin.

"What's going on, Mom?" Leah kept looking from me to Ali.

"Leah, please leave. Go back to the party." Ali's tone was clipped. Her cool composure was fading fast.

"But Mo—"

"Go, Leah. Now." Ali pinched the bridge of her nose.

Leah's eyes fell on me again, and I gave her an apologetic look. This wasn't how I had wanted to meet my little sister. My stomach did a little flip as I realized it. I was standing five feet away from my actual biological sister. She rolled her eyes at Ali but did as she was told and left.

"Alison, this is not how we treat guests in this family." The old lady lifted a handkerchief to her mouth and coughed several times before regaining composure.

Ali rushed to her grandmother's side and gave her an affectionate squeeze on the shoulder.

"G.G., why don't we get you to bed? It's getting late."

Ali moved to wheel her out of the room, but her grandmother held up her hand in protest.

"I may be dying, Alison, but I'm not dead yet." She shooed

Ali away and her eyes danced with amusement at the look of shock on her face. I was sure it mirrored my own. "Olivia will stay, and I would like to speak with her in private now."

I was either about to get some information or get executed. I wasn't sure which one I feared more.

"What could you possibly have to speak to a stranger about, G.G.?" Ali's tone was sweet, but her eyes were hard.

"Do you really want me to answer that, dear? Or shall we keep up the charade for appearance's sake?" G.G. had turned her neck to look back at Ali, who had transformed her expression into innocent curiosity.

Ali held her hand to her heart. "I didn't mean to offend you, G.G.," she murmured softly.

Wow, points for dramatic effect.

"I'll see you in a few minutes, Alison." There was a finality to the old woman's voice that could only come from being the matriarch of the family. Ali was done here, and we both knew it.

She stared daggers at me from behind her grandmother's wheelchair as though threatening me to stay silent, and then she quietly closed the door behind her.

9

"Would you like to have a seat, Olivia?"

The old lady gestured to the black leather couch I hadn't even noticed. Ali had left rather reluctantly, but staying had not been an option. My stomach clenched at not knowing what I was in for. I wrung my hands and shifted my weight from side to side as I took in the woman before me. She had the same green eyes as Ali, and therefore me as well, but where Ali's held a steely gaze, this woman's had a softness that made me feel hopeful despite myself. She was wearing a sparkly blue skirt and a topaz top with a pearl necklace and matching earrings. Though she was likely in her eighties, she had a youthful spirit about her. I nodded, not trusting myself to speak, and moved to sit on the couch.

"My name is Ruth, though I suppose you can call me Great Granny, or G.G. for short." She gave me a knowing smile.

My eyes grew wide, and my mouth was so dry all I could do was open and close it like some kind of trout.

"Yes, dear, I know who you are despite Alison's and my daughter Sheila's attempts to hide your existence from the world. You're seventeen now, yes?"

Again, I nodded. There was no trace of malice in her voice,

just pure honesty and perhaps a touch of sadness, but I couldn't be sure. My hands were folded neatly in my lap as though I wanted to convince this woman I was some kind of duchess. I tried to relax. *Maybe she knows who your birth father is.* The thought struck me so hard I nearly fell backwards.

"Do you—have you always known about me?" I changed my mind about asking her who my father was right off the bat. What if she felt the same way Ali did? I couldn't risk alienating this woman immediately. *Give it a few minutes at least.*

She didn't answer right away. Instead, she gave me a weak, pensive smile and grew quiet. A clock ticked somewhere in the room, and it sounded like a drum in my ears.

Tick, tick, tick. *You're not going to get the answers you came for.*

Tick, tick, tick. *Did you really think this woman would be the answer?*

Tick, tick, tick. *Why would she want to help you? You're not part of this family, remember?*

The last one stung, and I jolted. G.G. let out a sigh that sounded like it was mixed with hope, sadness, and a side of regret.

"I knew." She kept her head down, and when she looked up to meet my eyes, I was taken aback by the fact that hers were watering. "Can you ever forgive me, Olivia?"

The sorrow in her voice brought tears to my own eyes. I swallowed the lump that had formed in my throat.

"For what?" I whispered.

"I should have stepped in. I could have—should have helped. My husband, God rest his soul, was adamant that I stay out of it, but I knew it was wrong." She kneaded her fist against the arm of her wheelchair and looked off in the distance. "I kept track of you all this time. I felt as though it was not my place to step in when Sheila was so sure they were doing the right thing. But deep down I knew that we all could have helped. You were just a baby, for goodness' sake. For seventeen years I've been holding on to this apology. I am so sorry, Olivia." She dropped her gaze and fell still.

A warmth spread through my chest, and though I tried to fight it, a smile was slowly stretching across my face. I didn't have to wonder at her sincerity; I could feel it. I surprised myself by getting off the couch and kneeling in front of her.

"I forgive you, Ruth—G.G."

I looked up at her and bit the inside of my cheek to stop myself from full-on wailing once I saw the tears streaming down her face. Wordlessly she opened her arms wide, and I practically flung my head into her lap to let her embrace me. I heard the quiet sob escape her lips as she wrapped her arms around me, and I let the tears fall. We stayed like that—me kneeling in front of her, crying with my head in her lap; her with arms around me, silently sobbing—for a long, long time.

Eventually pins and needles began to pierce my legs and I was forced to get up. Ruth wiped her nose on the back of her hand unceremoniously. Our eyes met and we grinned at each other as I handed her some tissues from a box on the mahogany desk. We dabbed at our eyes while we composed ourselves.

"This is an answer to prayer, you know. Being able to apologize to you. Regret is such a terrible burden to live with." She patted my hand softly. "So…" She cleared her throat. "How can I help?"

I bit my lip. Would she understand?

"Well…" I lost my nerve immediately.

"Olivia, I don't imagine you would have braved showing up uninvited to a party like this without a good reason. Out with it." She wagged her finger at me and waited.

I blew my breath out. "Do you know who my birth father is?" It came out at a much higher pitch than I had intended, but it was out. No takebacks.

Her smile was sad. "I thought that might be it. I don't know a whole lot. They tried to keep it from me in the beginning."

My shoulders drooped as she tapped her temple. Then she

snapped her fingers and said, "Jason. That was his name, I'm sure of it."

My heart leapt at the sound. *It's only his first name, Liv, not a lot to go on.* Still, it was something. Much more than I had an hour ago.

"Thank you so much." My voice caught in my throat, and I cleared it.

"I'll do some digging, see what else I can find out." She rubbed her hands together mischievously.

"Oh, I can't ask you to do that. Ali would flip out. You've done so much—I don't want to cause more trouble than I already have."

She was already waving her hand dismissively. "You let me worry about Alison and your grandmother. I'm an old dying lady." She gave two pitiful fake coughs. "Who would suspect little ol' me?" She pumped her eyebrows twice, making me laugh out loud.

"Okay, okay." I put my hands up in defeat, then thought of something. "How will we get in touch with each other?"

"Ahhh yes, tricky. I could send up a smoke signal when I've found something." The twinkle in her eye made me realize how alike we were. "Or," she went on, "we could exchange cell phone numbers and I could just text you. Yes, even great-grandmothers in their eighties have cell phones."

I definitely liked her. We exchanged cell numbers, and she led me to a side door I hadn't seen.

"Probably best you sneak out without having to explain anything."

I turned to look at her and the sudden onslaught of emotion took me off guard. *What's wrong with you? You'll see her again.* She took my hands in hers and gently squeezed them.

"We'll see each other again, my sweet Olivia." She seemed to read my mind. She wiped away the tear that had slid down my cheek, and I let her cradle my face for a moment before I pulled away.

"Soon," I said hoarsely.

Once in the darkened hallway, I took a deep breath to steady myself. To the right were the bright lights of the rest of the house and the sounds of glasses clinking and guests laughing. To my left was a door that seemed to lead out to the side of the house. I was reaching for the handle when I heard it.

"What did she say to you?" I froze at the sound of Ali's voice behind me and thought fast. I couldn't, and wouldn't, betray my great-grandmother.

"Who's my birth father?" I countered, and angled my body so that I was still facing the door but just able to see her.

"You know I'm not going to tell you that." She folded her arms and narrowed her eyes.

"Likewise." I smiled to myself at the look on her face and walked out the door.

10

Two weeks later, the phone buzzed in my pocket as I was finishing my morning shift at Brew.

> I have information. Meet me at Tuscan Gardens in Delray. I'll leave a guest pass for you at the front desk. - G.G.R.

Ruth had insisted on code names to keep our anonymity intact. I was G.G.D.O. for "Great Granddaughter Olivia" and she was G.G.R. for "Great Granny Ruth." It wasn't exactly worthy of mission impossible, but it worked.

My pulse quickened as I reread the text a few times. This was what I had been waiting for. I knew where Tuscan Gardens was by heart at this point. It was the assisted living facility where Ruth lived, about forty minutes away from me. I had been visiting her every chance I got. I changed quickly in the back office into leggings and a green tank top and jumped in my car to make the familiar drive to Delray. I took the route that brought me along the ocean and watched the sunlight sparkle over the water for the entire drive. Once I arrived, I left the car in the visitors' parking lot and practically skipped up to the front desk.

"Good afternoon, Olivia." Olga, the facility manager, always greeted me warmly.

"Hi, Olga!"

She passed me my visitor's badge and I signed in.

"Where's the fire?" she called after me with a laugh as I rushed to G.G.

"I've got to reclaim my title as the reigning cribbage champion after Thursday's butt whooping," I called back to her as I swiped my guest badge along the panel and sped-walked through the main door.

G.G. was waiting for me in the common room, at our table by the large bay window overlooking the courtyard. Royal poinciana trees lined the interlocked walkways separated by mini palm trees. It was my new favorite view.

I strode over to where she was sitting in her wheelchair, wearing green shorts and a cream blouse. Leaning down, I hugged her tightly before sitting across from her and dealing the cards. A few other residents lazed about the room; some were playing cards, others were knitting, a couple were resting their eyes by the fireplace. The room was vast, with a cathedral ceiling that made it feel even bigger. Exposed wooden beams crisscrossed the entire ceiling, with an elaborate chandelier hanging at every few feet.

"How are you, Olivia? Have you made up with Lucas yet?" G.G.'s eyes sparkled as she made the first move in the game and the conversation.

Heat flooded my cheeks. "No, not yet."

"Why don't you follow him? See where he's going."

I raised my eyebrows. "That wouldn't be very ladylike, G.G."

She smiled at my words. "Sometimes we need to set our pride aside in order to get to the bottom of a mystery when it involves the ones we love." She raised a hand to flag down the waitress walking by and ordered a plate of shrimp with cocktail sauce and a cafe mocha. She balked at the look on my face. "Oh come now, dear. I've been on the planet far too long not to know what love looks like. You wouldn't be hurt if you didn't care so much."

I shifted in my seat uncomfortably as she made her next move in the game.

"How's Mela?" She'd changed the subject, but I wasn't sure which one was worse.

I stared at my cards for a long time before I answered with, "I'm honestly not sure."

She nodded empathetically, with decades of understanding behind her gaze. She reached across the table and put her hands over mine.

"Olivia, I've lived a long, beautiful life, which means I've lost loved ones and I've also been the one supporting dear friends losing theirs. Both are incredibly difficult in their own way." She patted my hand and pulled hers away.

"I just don't know how to be there for her. She keeps saying she's fine." I moved my peg five spots ahead.

"She's not fine." G.G.'s eyes were misty.

"What did *you* need when you were losing your mom?"

She smiled wistfully at my question. "I needed my best friend to just show up. To keep showing up even when I said I was fine. To sit with me, cry with me, scream with me. I just needed her presence. That's all Mela needs from you, Olivia. No guesswork, just you." Her eyes twinkled kindly at me.

I shifted in my seat. "So…" I started. She gave a little headshake and touched her finger to her lips. We waited while a lady hobbled by with her walker.

"Doris." G.G.'s—or Ruth's—lips were drawn tight.

"Ruth."

The contempt in their tone was palpable. I marveled at the fact that rivalry existed even well into old age and smiled into the café mocha the waitress had just set down in front of me.

"Oh, sweetie, some more sauce, please." Ruth was looking disdainfully at the rather small bowl of cocktail sauce before her.

"Ruth, you know I'm not supposed to give you too much cocktail sauce. It's full of sugar."

"Surely you wouldn't deny a little old lady her cocktail sauce. It could be my last meal!" G.G.'s mouth was turned down into a frown.

The waitress rolled her eyes and laughed as she walked back into the kitchen for more sauce.

"Now that that's handled, let's get down to business."

She speared a piece of shrimp with her fork, scooped it into the shrimp sauce, and popped it into her mouth. Her eyes closed for a moment as she savored it. I took another sip of my drink and waited with bated breath.

"I had to enlist some help, but I think we hit the jackpot." She pulled out a black and red leatherbound book from between her legs and looked from side to side as though it was contraband before sliding it across the table to me. I ran my fingers over the gold seal on the bottom right. *South Fork High School Yearbook* was embedded into the leather.

"This was Alison's yearbook from when she was a freshman. Jason was two or three years older than her, so I'm not sure which class he would be in, but I do believe they attended the same high school. There are a few thousand students in this yearbook, but he is most likely one of them."

My eyes glistened as I hugged the yearbook to my chest. "How did you get this?"

"As I said, I had some help." She winked mysteriously at me, and I knew that was all the information I was going to get.

I found myself driving to Mela's with G.G.'s words repeating in mind. *I needed my best friend to just show up.* I decided that I would do that. Just show up.

At her house, I discovered that the outside landscaping looked much better, which I took to be a good sign. Not long ago, it had begun to look like they were getting a jump on next year's Halloween decor.

The door swung open almost as soon as I knocked, and Mr. Moretti stood there, looking relieved to see me.

"Olivia! Wonderful timing. Could you sit with Renae while I run to the pharmacy to get her medication? Carmella is out on an errand and I don't want to wait on this."

He practically pulled me into the house as he grabbed his keys and left me standing in the hallway with my mouth hanging open. He was in his car and halfway down the street before I had collected myself and turned around.

"Mrs. Mor—Renae?" I called out into the seemingly empty house.

Silence met my question and sent a shiver down my spine. If he hadn't asked me to "sit with her" I would have stayed downstairs, but I couldn't just ignore his request. My eyes darted into the kitchen and my head snapped back a second time to take in the scene. Dishes were piled everywhere. The sink, the counter, the table, even inside the open microwave that evidently hadn't been cleaned in quite some time. There was a mop bucket half full of dirty water abandoned by the window and a pile of dirt on the floor covered by the broom resting against the fridge. I automatically took a step into the kitchen but stopped myself. I knew I had to keep going. I had to face whatever was waiting for me upstairs.

Slowly I climbed the stairs and hesitated in the open doorway to Renae's bedroom, unsure if I should walk through it or not. The moment I peeked my head in, my eyes bulged and my jaw dropped.

Piles of unfolded laundry lay all over the room. Dirty plates and bowls were stacked and ready to be taken downstairs, and a thick layer of dust covered the mirror over the dresser. The smell of disinfectant was pungent in my nostrils, and I could hear the low hum of a lawnmower crisscrossing back and forth over the grass in the background. A couch I didn't recognize was covered with crumpled sheets and blankets and had been pulled into the room directly beside the bed. The king-sized four-poster bed I was used to had been replaced by an electric hospital-grade bed with rails, just large enough for one person.

My eyes focused and refocused on the bed, and I couldn't make sense of what I was seeing. When I did, I had to keep myself from gasping in shock. *How long has it been since I was here?* I did the mental math even as I stared at the familiar woman before me, who had become unrecognizable.

She was propped up in bed against several pillows and her hair, once long and lustrous, was now so thin that I could see her scalp. Her eye sockets had sunk into her face and were barely visible thanks to the circles under them that were so black I almost wondered if someone had drawn on her with a sharpie. She was lying on top of the covers with a light pale-yellow blanket covering her lower half while her exposed arms appeared skeletal.

I bit my lip hard, as I now understood how much Mela had been lying to me for the last several weeks while I distracted myself with the search for Jason. I was so obsessed with finding him that I had been happy to believe Mela when she said everything was fine. I was worried about not finding him in time when all the while Mela had been dealing with an even greater tragedy right under my nose.

"Olivia…"

I jumped at the hoarse sound of my name and realized I was still standing in the doorway, and Renae was staring at me.

With the sting of tears behind my eyelids, I blinked quickly as I tiptoed closer to her bed.

"Hi, Renae." It came out as a squeak.

"Pretty intense, huh?"

She winced as she shifted ever so slightly and patted the bed beside her. I sat down as gently as possible and lifted one knee to my chest for support while my other foot stayed securely on the floor.

"You look…great," I said.

I tried to smile but the muscles in my face wouldn't cooperate, and I was sure it looked more like a grimace.

"Liar." She chuckled softly as her eyes searched my face. "What's that you got there?" I looked down and realized I was still holding the yearbook.

"It's-it's my birth mother's yearbook. I think my birth father might be in it, so I came to see if Mela wanted to help me look…" I trailed off. *Why hasn't Mela told me how bad it's gotten?* More rapid blinking as I faked interest in the carpet.

"That's great," she whispered. "Carmella will need the distraction." Her eyes closed for a long moment and mine flew to her chest, to make sure it was still rising and falling.

"No, no I wouldn't dream of pulling her focus away right now, Renae." I moved to touch her hand, but she looked so fragile I didn't trust myself not to hurt her.

"Olivia, she needs you now more than ever. I'm not making it out of this alive and I don't want my daughter to watch me die slowly. Promise me you'll get her out of the house for more than a chemo run to the pharmacy."

The breath caught in my throat. *No, she can't be serious. She's going to make it.* What I found in her face was a resignation that made me squirm. She knew she was going to die and now I knew it too. I couldn't blink back the tears any longer and a strangled sob escaped my lips. Renae's hand gently caressed my face and wiped the tears away as they fell.

"Promise me." Her voice was thick with emotion.

I couldn't speak, and yet I had to. "I…I…prom…ise." I hiccupped through the words as the tears continued to fall.

She lifted her arm, and I took the invitation to nestle into her as she gently rubbed my back the way she had done a thousand times before.

"I"—she cleared her throat and went on—"I love you, Olivia.

You are the best bonus daughter I could have hoped for." She paused to take some gulps of air while I openly sobbed into the mattress. "I'm sorry that your birth mother can't see how amazing you are, but I feel so blessed to have been a part of your life all these years. You are worth it. I hope you realize that someday."

"I…wish...you had…more time." Once the words were out, I wailed, and my stomach tightened as the sobs wracked my body.

I heard her whisper, "Me too." And then there was silence.

After a while I could hear light snores coming from her, and I gently moved off the bed. I could still hear the lawnmower, so I tiptoed over to the window to tap on the glass and ask whoever was outside to stop. I glanced down at the lawn and saw a tall young man with dirty blond hair, and then I noticed the black truck parked out front. I dropped to the floor; it was Lucas.

He's the one who's been taking care of their landscaping? Damn, that was just so…Lucas. The familiar longing for his arms settled deep in my stomach. I leaned on my knees and snuck another peek. Mr. Moretti had just pulled up and walked over to Lucas. They glanced up at the window and I dropped down again. I crawled the length of the room to sit on the floor across from Renae's bed, hoping they hadn't seen me. It felt like some kind of spy movie; theme music should have been playing in the background. I heard Mr. Moretti open and close the front door, and a couple of minutes later he stepped into the room.

"Thank you for staying, Olivia."

He squeezed my shoulder. I looked up at him and smiled sadly. He looked weary in a way I didn't ever want to be. There were no adequate words to express my sorrow, so I simply squeezed his hand and nodded, then picked up the pile of dishes to take to the kitchen as I left. Lucas was doing his part, and I wanted to do mine.

I glanced at Mela's bedroom door, and I swelled with admiration for her. The way she was pressing on through this was so courageous. She wasn't being a coward by keeping this from me, and I needed to let her go through this however she wanted to. I would be there for all of it.

I snuck down the stairs and stopped at the halfway point to look out the round window at the landing. Lucas's muscles glistened in the sun. Somehow, over the last few weeks he had become even more beautiful. I watched as he finished with the lawn and moved over to weed the gardens. Where had he been all this time? Why the secrecy?

I forced myself to walk down the rest of the stairs. Once I got into the kitchen, I started tidying up. I loaded the dishwasher as I kept an eye on Lucas from the kitchen window. I was far enough away that he couldn't see me, but I could see him perfectly. Too perfectly. It made me think of the date we had had on the beach and talking well into the night.

"I miss you," I whispered.

He stood up from the gardens then started packing the lawnmower into his truck.

Why don't you follow him? See where he's going. G.G.'s words floated through my mind. I made the split second decision to do just that. I was tired of living in limbo, and I was going to get to the bottom of it today.

11

I carefully followed Lucas's truck, staying far behind for him not to notice. Part of me was worried he was just going to head back to Nate's, but within a couple of minutes I knew he wasn't heading home.

My heart thudded as I tracked him into a shadier part of town. I never spent time there if I could help it, but I was determined to know where he was going. It seemed as though every second house was boarded up and had dirt instead of grass for a lawn. Most driveways were either gravel or cracked pavement, and no parked vehicle looked operational. My fingers tapped nervously against the steering wheel, and I was just about to abandon the mission when I saw him do a U-turn and park on the other side of the street. I immediately pulled off the road and parked closely behind another car, hoping it would shield me enough.

I didn't need to worry that he would see me. He was so focused on the house across the street that he would have never noticed anything else. What was he doing? My eyebrows were so furrowed I could practically see them. There was something niggling at the edge of my subconscious. The house he was watching looked more like a trailer, and I could just make out what looked like beer bottles thrown around the dirt lawn. The paint on the front of the trailer was chipping so badly that large chunks had fallen off. A rusted-out Honda Civic hatchback sat on the gravel driveway with a flat tire and a smashed window.

My eyes darted from Lucas to the house, back and forth, back and forth. What had Mela said that day? *Think Liv, think.* And then it all came back to me.

"Lucas doesn't live in the greatest neighborhood, so I wanted to get out of there fast, ya know? I pulled up to his house and… the paint was super faded and chipped, there was a junky car in the driveway and I could hear screaming from inside the house…"

I snatched my purse from the passenger seat and rifled through it until I found my phone. My hands were shaking as I furiously typed a message to Mela.

That time you picked Lucas up from his mom's house, was it on Fischer Street?

I chewed the inside of my cheek as I waited for her answer, my nails still drumming against the top of my dashboard. My phone buzzed a minute later.

Yeah, I think so. Why?

My spirits sank. I wanted to be wrong, but I wasn't.

Tell you later. Thanks.

I guess he's not cheating on me. How long had he been watching his mom's house? And why wouldn't he just have told me that? After a moment, I called him as I stepped out of my car. I watched him look down and immediately put the phone to his ear.

"Liv? Are you okay?" He sounded worried.

"Why, because I'm calling first?" I grimaced.

"Well…yeah."

"Can we talk?" I was almost at his truck, but he hadn't noticed me yet. His eyes were still on his mom's house.

"Of course. Just tell me when and where."

"Here and now is good." I tapped on his passenger window, which made him jump and drop his phone. He threw me a weary gaze and unlocked his truck. I clambered in and our eyes met. For a minute we didn't say anything.

"What are you doing here?" We said it in unison.

He rested the back of his head against the rest. "You first."

All of a sudden, I didn't feel so confident. I hadn't thought about having to explain why I was in front of his mother's house. I wiped my sweaty palms on my capris.

"I…followed you from Mela's." I stared at the glovebox and heard him shift in his seat.

"Oh."

"How long have you been taking care of their yard?" My eyes were still trained on the glovebox.

"Does it really matter?"

"It matters to me," I murmured.

"Since the day after you told me her mom was sick. I drove by and saw how bad it was, so I took care of it. I figured it was one less thing for them to worry about."

That thoughtfulness lay at the core of who Lucas was—but I couldn't ease the pressure now. "Your turn to tell me why you're here." When he said nothing, I urged, "Come on, Lucas. I already know you've been staking out your mom's house. You can at least tell me why?"

"I'm worried about her," he said, overcoming his hesitation. "She has a nasty habit of dating violent douchebags, and my brother told me she has started dating someone new. At least when I lived here I could step in—but I was tired of her choosing her boyfriends over her kids, so I left."

"But you can't just abandon her." Savior Lucas, always

looking out for others. "Why didn't you just tell me? You really could have saved us a lot of heartache."

"You don't get it."

"What don't I get, Lucas? Explain it to me."

He huffed and got out, slamming the door behind him. I followed suit and we faced off in front of his truck.

"Do you see this place?" He waved his arm angrily at the trailer. "You live in a nice neighborhood with parents who don't beat each other, and you went to *Gibbons*." I cringed at the way he said my old high school's name.

"So what?"

"So *what*? I'm trash, Liv. I come from trash. I thought if you saw this place and knew where I came from…you'd know it too. You're too good for me and I just…I didn't want to lose you." His voice cracked on the last word, and he looked away.

I shook my head in disbelief. How could I ever think this beautiful boy was trash? The very thought was offensive. I stepped toward him, wrapped my arms around his waist, and pressed my head against his chest. He stiffened at first and then I felt him melt into me and squeeze me closer. I thought of the way he fought Chris off last year. The way he was willing to go to jail so I wouldn't have to face that psycho. I thought of how he'd pulled me out of the ocean and let me cry on his shoulder without a word. And now he was mowing Mela's lawn though we weren't even speaking.

"You're not trash, Lucas. You're the furthest thing from it." I squeezed his waist a little tighter and he rested his chin on top of my head. "Do you want to get out of here?"

"Yeah. But first…"

I looked up at him questioningly. He tilted my chin up and whispered, "I missed you" just before he pressed his lips to mine.

A few hours later we were sitting with Nate and Mela on Nate's living room couch, poring over Ali's yearbook with post-it-notes and sticky tabs, looking for every Jason we could find.

There were over three thousand students at the school that year, so it was slow going. The only thing we knew for sure was that my father was African American, which helped to narrow it down, but we still had to find every single student with that name and description. In the end, we found sixty-two Jasons. Thirty-seven between grades eleven and twelve, twenty-nine without glasses since I had perfect eyesight, and only seven who were African American.

As I watched my friends flip through the pages and take copious notes just to help me, I couldn't wipe the smile off my face. Lucas and I were sitting close to each other; his arm was around my shoulders and his fingers twirled my hair.

I snuck a glance at Mela for the tenth time in five minutes. She added another note to the sheet we were working on, and I realized that this was what she needed: friends, laughter, a distraction. I had to let her be and just support whichever way she chose to process her sorrow. I tried to communicate, in our telepathic way after seventeen years of friendship, that I was there for her, however she needed. She smiled and gave me a slight nod. Message received.

Nate stood up to make a snack.

"Liv, can I get your help?" I hated to tear myself away from Lucas, but I jumped up and followed him into the kitchen.

He walked to the cupboard and pulled out a bag of plain Ruffles, so I opened the fridge and grabbed the unopened onion dip. I smiled to myself. Some things never changed.

"Liv, I'm sorry I couldn't tell you what he was really doing." Nate was leaning against the kitchen island, looking worried. "I tried to convince him to tell you. I knew you wouldn't think he was trash. I've known you for years, and judging someone for the family they were born into—it just isn't you. Can you forgive me for not telling you?" His eyes shone with sincerity.

"I wasn't fair to you, Nate. I put you in an impossible situation, and I'm sorry for that. Obviously, you're forgiven." I hugged him, and he spun me around once as we laughed before setting me down.

Lucas and Mela came into the kitchen. Life was good: Lucas and I were inseparable again, Mela was smiling, and Nate and I had made up. In the back of my mind, I knew that a hundred things still could and would rip our hearts out but, in that moment, I set them all aside and decided to steal a moment of happiness—however fleeting it might be.

12

Armed with their last names and having flagged their respective pages, Lucas and I drove to Tuscan Gardens two days later to see if Ruth recognized any of the Jasons since she had met him at a few family dinners.

"Here." Lucas grinned as soon as I sat beside him in the truck and handed me my favorite giant marble cupcake loaded with French vanilla icing as well as a beautiful red box wrapped with a sparkly bow.

"Mmmm." I scooped some icing into my mouth. "What's this, though?" I eyed the red box like it was a ticking time bomb.

"I saw it and thought of you. Just open it, it won't bite," he suggested as we drove by a guy in a black Range Rover who was jamming out to his music so hard that he swerved and had to collect himself before continuing his drum solo on his steering wheel.

"I'll do it after my cupcake."

I slowly peeled the wrapper back. I had never enjoyed opening gifts in front of people. My poker face was nonexistent, and it had made for some awkward moments in the past.

"I can't believe you didn't tell me about going to Ali's party."

Lucas's eyes darted over at me for a second before focusing back on the road.

"Well, we weren't exactly on speaking terms." I leaned against my headrest and pretended to watch the water as I studied his face. It felt like I hadn't seen him in ages.

"I still would have gone with you."

"I know."

Smiling, I brushed his hair out of his eyes and slid the back of my hand down the side of his face. He grabbed it and pressed it to his lips. I sighed happily as we pulled off the highway, and before I knew it, we were parking in visitor's parking at Tuscan Gardens. I could feel him watching me.

"Okay, okay. I'll open it." I fumbled with the box and sucked in my breath when I finally pulled off the lid. "Lucas…" Lying on satin within the box was a delicate gold necklace with a sparkly diamond-encrusted starfish pendant.

"May I?" He was reaching for the box.

I nodded and turned, having lost the ability to speak for the moment while I held my hair up and he fastened it behind my neck. He gently kissed my exposed shoulder, making me shiver and lean back against him for support.

"Thank you." My words were barely audible, but I felt him smile.

We got out of the truck, and I fiddled with my hair as we walked up to the door.

"Are you nervous?" he asked. How did he know that I tucked my hair behind my ears when I was nervous?

"No. Well…maybe a little?"

What if they don't like each other? I knew it was stupid, but the thought was there anyway. What if the magic between G.G. and me only existed in our little bubble? Lucas pulled me close and kissed my forehead.

"You're adorable."

I pulled him through the door, fingering my necklace and smiling to myself. Olga was standing in front of her desk as though she had been waiting for me. The look on her face stopped me in my tracks.

"She's not—" I couldn't finish.

"She's okay." Olga put her hands up quickly as she approached. "But I can't let you see her."

I was so relieved that G.G. was okay that I didn't fully comprehend what Olga had said.

"What do you mean?" My hands had begun trembling.

"Olivia, I'm so sorry, but your visitation rights have been revoked. I can't let you in to see her." Olga's expression was pained.

"Revoked? That doesn't make any sense. I'll just text her." I pulled out my phone and sent her a quick text. I knew she'd clear everything up.

Message failed.

Failed? Unease was growing in the pit of my stomach. I tried again with the same result. I pressed the phone icon to call her.

"I'm sorry. The number you have dialed is not in service at this time. Please try your call again. This is a recording."

The robotic voice was like nails down a chalkboard in my mind. Disconnected? I had just spoken to her a couple of days ago. How could it be disconnected? I looked up at Lucas helplessly and felt my cheeks grow warm. *She must have changed her mind about me.* I forced a smile as I met Olga's sympathetic eyes.

"Who revoked her visitation rights?" Lucas was still beside me, and his voice flat. I turned to tell him that it didn't matter, but Olga was already responding.

"Her daughter. I'm-I'm so sorry, Olivia."

Her daughter. Her *daughter*? Sheila had done this?

"But-but why? How did she even kn—"

My eyes fell on the logbook I signed at every visit. I ran my finger down the list until I found my name, and five spaces below was Sheila Schafer's name. She had visited yesterday and must have seen my name on it. Olga leaned back on her feet and shook her head, probably at my misfortune, then she backed away and returned to her seat behind the glass partition, removing my ability to ask any further questions.

I turned on my heels and stormed out the door with Lucas trailing behind me. What if I never got to see G.G. again? She was dying, for goodness' sake, and I'd never even gotten a chance to say goodbye.

Damn you, Ali. This has your name written all over it.

Back at the truck, I yanked open the door—but before I could get in, my phone rang.

"Mom?" My forehead scrunched together. "I'm just out with Lucas…umm yeah, I can be home in like forty minutes…is everyth—" She had hung up.

"What now?" Lucas sounded as weary as I felt.

"I don't know, but I need to get home. I think I'm in trouble." My heart was racing.

"You don't think it's about…" Lucas gestured to the building we'd just left.

"How could it be?"

Even as I said it, though, I wasn't so sure. Would Ali really go that far?

I reread the letter that had been sent by registered mail to my mom's office. I couldn't make sense of what I was reading. Words like "cease and desist" and "no contact" seemed to float off the page and slap me in the face. What did it all mean?

"How long, Olivia?"

My mom's tone made me jolt. The impatience in it led me to think this wasn't the first time she had asked, but I had no idea what she was saying.

"How long what?" I looked down and let my hair fall in front of my face like a shield, the way I used to when I was a child.

"How long have you been searching for your birth father?" She paced back and forth across the kitchen floor.

The laminate was coming up in some spots. Dirt had clung to the cracks where it had lifted, and the diamond pattern was so faded in some places that it was hardly visible. Her socked feet came into view, and I looked up. She was standing directly in front of me, eyes blazing.

"Since last year after meeting Ali."

"So, when you wanted your birth certificate and asked about the redacted letter it wasn't for a doctor's appointment, was it?"

"No, it wasn't." No sense lying at this point.

"You lied to my face, Olivia!" She threw her hands in the air and started pacing again while muttering to herself under her breath. I could only understand every few words. "Unbelievable…how could she…so embarrassed…running all over town…completely ungrateful…"

I winced.

"So let me get this straight"—she held one finger in the air—"you crashed Ali's fourth of July party"—a second finger—"trespassed onto private property" —a third finger— "and have been visiting her *dying* grandmother *without* permission, possibly *jeopardizing* her health. Is that about right?" Her nostrils flared as she continued to hold her fingers in the air while her thumb covered her pinky.

"Well, it's not *exactly* right…" I shuffled my feet as I heard the front door open and shut. My dad's dirty work boots came into view. *Crap.*

"What's so important that I had to leave work early?" He huffed impatiently, and at each glance I snuck, his eyes grew wider and wider as my mom filled him in.

"Olivia." His voice was low and grave.

"Look, I'm sorry, but Ali is blowing this way out of proportion." My hand clutched the cease-and-desist letter so tightly I thought it might disintegrate.

"This is really serious. A no-contact order for her entire

family? What's gotten into you?" he demanded. His hands were on his hips and his head cocked to the side in utter disbelief. His lips were pulled so tight they were turning white.

A trail of ants was making off with some crumbs. *Take me with you,* I called after them in my head. They could carry many times their weight or something, couldn't they? Maybe if enough of them banded together, I could just drop to the floor and let them drag me away. The absurdity of the thought almost made me smile, which would not have been a good thing, given the gravity of my situation.

"Olivia, are we not enough for you?"

My mother's words seemed to hang in midair as I sucked in my breath through my teeth. Her eyes bore into mine and pleaded with me. She looked so fragile I was almost afraid to speak. Shame flooded me, and I wanted to take it all back. Maybe I should have told them everything. Maybe I should have asked for permission. I was filled with a regret so deep it threatened to consume me and yet...

"That's not fair," I whispered. Searching for my birth father had nothing to do with them. I cringed as my dad wrapped his arms around her shoulders as though protecting her from the pain I was causing her—*from me.*

"You need to give up the search. Do you hear me? You're done looking for him." My father was livid.

"Dad—"

He lifted his hand to stop me. "You're also grounded." He was still shielding my mom from me.

"*Grounded*? For searching for my birth father?"

"No, Olivia, for lying to us about being at work when you were in fact trespassing on private property and crashing a party you had absolutely no business being at." He had now adopted the scary kind of calm that made me want to run screaming from the room.

"You're only seventeen, Olivia! You can't be getting into situations like this." My mom's voice was muffled by my dad's chest.

I stood in the kitchen, staring at the ants until my parents realized I wasn't going to say another word. They stormed off to their room to discuss the details of my punishment. I stayed in the same spot until it was too dark for me to see, and then I went to my room.

Now I had to get creative—because though I didn't want to add stress to their lives, I also had no intention of calling off the search.

13

Sometimes when things start to fall apart, it's always wise to patch up what you can. That being said, no one has ever accused me of being all that wise.

"Coach!" I called out as I walked from the parking lot over to the track in shorts and a tank top, ready to run just in case.

The familiar red rubber called to me. The smell of the freshly cut grass and the sounds of birds were soothing. A few team members were already warming up with a light jog around the track while the rest of the team trickled in. It was a beautiful, sunny September day but somehow I felt a chill as Coach Addison turned and gave me a withering look.

"Jackson," he grumbled.

"Coach Addison, I think it's time for me to rejoin the team." I puffed out my chest to appear more confident than I felt.

"Is that so?" He was now looking at a clipboard and checking things off with a pen.

"Yes, sir." I faltered a little as I said it.

He looked up and met my eyes. "It's been weeks, Jackson. Why do I get the feeling you didn't tell your parents what happened here?" His face was twisted into a knowing smirk.

And I'm not telling you they grounded me either. I sighed, didn't deny it, and said, "I'm really sorry about before. I'm ready to get my head back in the game."

I waited patiently as he pulled his black baseball cap farther down his face and folded his arms. His eyes narrowed at me as I quietly waited for his answer.

"It's not gonna be easy, Jackson. If you thought I was hard on you before, that's going to look like child's play in comparison. You sure you're up for that?"

Oh, gosh, he's going to enjoy this. My stomach dropped.

"Yes, sir." I said it much more enthusiastically than I felt. I nearly gave him a salute but worried he might take it for sarcasm. Which it would be.

"Then get to it, Jackson. This is gonna be fun."

He nodded to the track, and I didn't give him time to change his mind. I started a light jog and fell in beside Felicity. She smiled politely at me.

"Good to have you back, Olivia." And then she picked up the pace and left me in the dust.

Yeah, this is gonna be fun.

"What can I get started for you?" I smiled at the young mom attempting to wrangle her screaming toddler back into her arms.

"Coffee. Preferably hooked up to my veins."

She dropped a five-dollar bill on the counter and ran to scoop up her son who had—in ten seconds—managed to run to the other side of the room and begin pulling books off the bookshelf. He was chucking them with such fervor that it almost looked like an exorcism in a horror movie, where books inexplicably fly off the shelf. I poured her coffee in a to-go cup and smirked at Lucas, who was sitting at a table with my laptop and the yearbook, shaking his head in disbelief.

I wasn't allowed to hang out with Lucas officially, but they couldn't very well stop him from visiting me at work. I walked over to him and dropped into a chair, leaning the crook of my arm on the table.

You're working too much." He reached across the table and ruffled my hair.

"What else am I supposed to do? It's this, track practice, or home." I winced as I pictured my dad standing protectively between my mom and me.

"Still, how many hours have you worked since school started back up?"

"I'm not totally sure," I lied. Sixty-five hours in two weeks. It was the most I'd ever worked in a pay period, and I couldn't even go anywhere to spend my check.

Pursing his lips, he didn't say anything. I pulled his notebook to my side of the table and flipped it open.

Jason Chelmy
Jason Harris
~~Jason Hawkins~~
Jason Pritchard
~~Jason Redding~~
~~Jason Smythe~~
Jason Wilkes

"Who's up today?" I rubbed my temples in a circular motion.

It was slow going. We had been looking for each Jason through social media and Google, but it was challenging when there were so many men with the same name. We had sent dozens of messages, left voicemails, and had even gotten a hold of a few Jasons on the phone, but I learned rather quickly that it wasn't as simple as just asking if they had had a child seventeen years earlier. After Jason Hawkins' wife started screaming in the background and accusing him of having an affair, we decided that more discretion was necessary.

"Why don't we take a break from this, Liv?" Lucas closed the laptop and reached for my hand. "You're stressed, and I don't think this is helping."

"It's more important now than ever. Obviously, I have no hope of having a relationship with anyone in Ali's family. I'm running out of time." I got up to serve a customer who had come in while we were talking.

There was an urgency within me that had been building for some time. I didn't know why exactly, but I knew I had to find him soon. Just as I sat back down with Lucas, my phone rang. I pulled it out but didn't recognize the number.

"Hello?"

"Olivia? It's Mark Riker." I wracked my brain, trying to identify him, but I was drawing a blank. "I'm Ali's husband."

My jaw dropped. "Oh! Umm, hi?" *Smooth, Liv, really.*

"I'm in town on business and I was wondering if we could meet." He sounded strong and confident.

"I'm not really sure Ali would like that, considering the no-contact order." I spoke slowly and with hesitation. Was this a trap? If it was, I didn't want to get caught in it.

"Ali won't know about this." He paused and waited for my reply.

"Okay… Well, I'm at work, so you can come see me here if you want. I'm here for another two hours." I held my breath.

"Text me the address. I'm on my way."

I only blew out my breath as I hung up.

Forty-five minutes later I sat across from Mark at one of the private booths in the back of Brew. Jenna was manning the shop for me so we could speak privately, and Lucas was doing a terrible job of pretending he wasn't listening. Mark looked just like his picture. He was much taller than I was—at least six feet—had salt-and-pepper hair and wore a gray business suit, while drinking a raspberry-pomegranate tea. His kind blue eyes and friendly smile put me at ease.

"Olivia, it's nice to meet you. I want to start out by saying how sorry I am for the way Ali has handled this entire situation."

He took a sip of his tea while I collected myself. He was apologizing to *me*?

"Umm, okay. I'm sorry, Mark, I'm having a hard time understanding why you're here. Why would you risk her…*wrath* just to talk to me?"

My cappuccino sat untouched in front of me. Mark chuckled as he rubbed his chin thoughtfully. Our eyes met and his twinkled.

"Ali may seem scary to you, but I think she's just scared."

"Scared? Of what?" I thought of every time I had seen her. Calm, cool, collected. Never scared.

"Honestly, I'm not totally sure." He leaned forward as though about to tell me a secret and went on. "She doesn't really talk about her life before me. But to answer your question, my parents divorced when I was young, and my mom refused to let me see my dad. I always resented her for it."

Out of the corner of my eye I saw Lucas shift and lean in.

Mark continued talking. "I just don't think that any parent has the right to stop their child from seeing the other parent. I promised myself a long time ago that I would never do that, and I can't just sit by while my wife does it to you." He pulled an old, already opened envelope out of his pocket and slid it across the table. I didn't pick it up immediately but instead took a nervous sip of my coffee. He nodded toward the envelope.

"I found this in the same box as Ali's yearbooks. It's a letter to her from your birth father, from when she was pregnant with you."

The quick look I threw him managed to be surprised and grateful all at once. "I don't even know what to say. Thank you so much." He smiled. "Wait, so *you* gave Ruth the yearbook?"

Mark tipped an imaginary hat at me. "Guilty. Oh, and I will try to talk Sheila into reinstating your visitation rights to see Ruth, but don't hold your breath. Ali has her mother wrapped around her finger." He checked his watch and got to his feet. "If I find anything else, I'll pass it on to you. Good luck, Olivia."

As I thanked him again, Mark squeezed my shoulder and then left me to my thoughts.

"Are you going to look at that?" Lucas's voice pulled me back to reality.

He had slid into Mark's place in the booth and was pointing at the envelope in front of me. It was face down; I touched it gently and flipped it over.

In the top left corner of the envelope was the name of the return sender: Jason Pritchard.

Lucas's eyes shone with excitement as I grinned at him. This was what we'd been searching for. We finally knew my father's last name.

14

The very next day, Mela's mom died.

The funeral was by far the saddest thing I had ever been to. It was held in the Catholic Church where Mela's parents had married. So many people came to celebrate the life of a woman who was clearly loved. The four of us sat in the front row holding hands. Lucas held my hand, I held Mela's, and she held Nate's.

I watched her dad walk up to the front of the room so slowly I wasn't sure he would make it. He tapped the microphone gently and began the eulogy.

"Renae was a special person: she must have been, to put up with me for so long. We met in high school, and she was the love of my life for thirty years. She was the most beautiful girl I had ever seen, and to my shock she loved this scrawny freshman right back."

His voice grew thick, and he cleared his throat before continuing.

"Her reputation of kindness preceded her everywhere she went. A day didn't pass when I didn't pinch myself and wonder why someone like her would choose someone like me. She exuded a radiance that cast a glow on everything and everyone around her.

"Her most treasured legacy is our daughter, Carmella. I have never seen a mother love her daughter as much as Renae loved Carmella. She was so proud of you, sweetheart."

He choked back a sob as he looked over at Mela, and I squeezed her hand.

"We were supposed to grow old together. That was the plan. Grandchildren and rocking chairs on our front porch in the country while we watched the storms and discussed how much we needed the rain."

He smiled sadly to himself as though remembering a joke they'd shared. My chest felt like lead as I recalled the many times I had heard them talk about those very plans. *This isn't fair.*

"I never could have imagined that she would be ripped away from me, from Carmella, from her parents and siblings so soon. We should have had fifty more years together, and it still wouldn't have been enough."

His voice now trembled, and I knew he wasn't going to make it for much longer.

"Renae is not really gone. The smell of coffee reminds me of starting the morning with her. The flowerbeds lining the driveway remind me that she would be there, wearing her hat and gardening gloves and waving me goodbye in the morning. The light that Carmella remembers to switch on in the porch reminds me that Renae would be there to kiss me hello. I've been told I should give away her things now or it will be even more painful later, but how can it be more painful? So many scarves and sweaters still smell like her…

"And yet I already know that it's true she hasn't died. I was going through the plans for today and telling them to her. She would say she loved these flowers, loved the music, but that I shouldn't make my speech too long, and I shouldn't make Mela cry," he looked over at his daughter and both sobbed once, and then smiled.

"So I'm gonna stop now. I want to get home and tell her how it went. Tell her that all her friends were here, and they'll all remember her too. I know I won't be alone. She will always be with me."

There wasn't a dry eye in the building. My face hurt from the sheer volume of the tears I wept. They came from a place I didn't know existed.

After the funeral there was a reception at Mela's for close friends and family. As soon as one of her cousins referred to it as the "lame afterparty," the four of us escaped to Mela's bedroom to save me from having to explain why I'd assaulted one of the bereaved.

I closed the door behind me and caught Mela's eye. She had a wide grin on her face and was stifling a laugh.

"Mela!" I gasped, which completely set her off.

"You should have seen your face!"

She was doubled over, arms wrapped around her stomach, openly cackling while she gasped for air. I felt a flush creep across my cheeks. I looked at Lucas for support, but he was conveniently staring out the window, though I could have sworn I saw his shoulders shaking ever so slightly.

"You think this is...*funny*?" I glanced at Nate, who was sitting on Mela's bed, staring at the floral comforter with an unmistakable smirk on his face.

"My mom being dead?" Mela asked. "No, of course not. But I think it's freaking hilarious that he called it an afterparty. Like what was he expecting? Strobe lights and a DJ?"

Lucas snorted. A laugh bubbled up and escaped my lips as my hand flew over my mouth. My stomach started shaking, and before I could stop it, I was doubled over, holding myself up with my hands on my knees and laughing so hard that tears were streaming down my face.

"Oh my gosh, this is so wrong, but I can't stop laughing!"

I was now on the floor, gasping through the pain of laughing so hard. Eventually we pulled ourselves together, and Mela's laughter instantly turned to tears. I crawled over to where she was sitting on the floor and wrapped my arm around her shoulder, pulling her close. Nate moved from the bed quickly to sit on her other side and Lucas came to sit beside me.

"She was the best." My voice cracked on the last word.

"What did she say to you that day?" Mela asked through her sniffles.

I fell still. *You are worth it. I hope you realize that someday.* Her words replayed in my mind, but I wasn't sure what they meant. What was "it" supposed to be? For the moment, that conversation was just for Renae and me—so I chose to tuck it into my heart to explore it another day.

"She told me that I was the best bonus daughter she could have hoped for." It was mostly the truth.

Mela nodded. "She really did love you like a daughter."

My throat tightened at her words. *The wrong woman died. It should have been Ali.* I flushed with immediate regret. *That was dark, Liv, really dark.* I shrugged, trying to rid myself of the guilt.

"What happened with Mark yesterday?" Mela was blowing her nose with a tissue.

"Oh, it was nothing. It doesn't matter right now," I said quickly.

Lucas tilted his head disapprovingly, and I threw him a look. I wasn't about to tell my best friend that I was closer to finding my father when she had just lost her mom.

"Liv. I know my mom made you promise to distract me during and after her death." She held up her finger to stop me from speaking, so I closed my mouth. "I know because she made me promise her something too."

"What?" I finally asked when the silence had stretched on for longer than I could handle.

"That I would let you."

Our eyes met and I saw the fierce determination behind hers, as though she were saying, "This will not break me." I admired her grit, even if it did feel completely wrong to be discussing this with a house full of grieving people downstairs. Lucas nodded his encouragement, and I brought her and Nate up to speed.

"So, you have his last name? Wow." Nate gave a low whistle as he processed the news.

"Have you started looking? What was the return address on the envelope?"

Mela's eyes were dry, and I could see that shifting her focus to our investigation was indeed helping to take her mind off her mom; mine too.

"It wasn't a real address, just a P.O. Box." I had hoped that it would be his parents' address and I could just waltz on over and ask for his whereabouts, but it wasn't going to be that simple.

"Hmm, okay. Well, we just need to start looking for every Jason Pritchard there is." She stood up and walked over to sit at her desk, where she turned her computer on.

"Mel, we don't have to start right this second."

"Would you rather I throw myself on my bed and weep for the rest of my life? Trust me, I want to. And I will. But I want to do that privately. Not with a house full of distant relatives who consider my mother's death an inconvenience to their party plans." She turned back to her Mac, and I let her.

There would be time to grieve later, and maybe that was how grief worked. Maybe the way to truly recover from the most unimaginable kind of heartache was through pockets of time. Perhaps dealing with the grief all at once would crush Mela, and instead she needed to be able to tuck it away safely, only taking it out during fragments when she was ready for it. The rest of the time she needed to live her life so that the despair wouldn't consume her. If this was how she needed to process her grief, I was here for it—and for her.

15

"Let me read it again."

Mela held out her hand for the letter from Jason. It was the fourth time in an hour. We were holed up in my room, hiding from my parents. Mela was the only exception to the no-guest rule, and she was tired of sitting at home alone while her dad worked overtime. I handed her the letter again and she read it out loud.

Ali,

I'm begging you to reconsider. You won't take my calls, so I've had to resort to registered mail. Rose is my daughter too, please don't shut me out like this. I can get my life together enough for her. Please, if you don't want her then I do. She's my baby, and I have the right to keep her.

Jase

"Ugh, there just aren't any clues in this."

She put the letter down on my bed. I picked it up and tucked it away in my secret drawer. There was no way I wanted to let my parents find that letter. It would raise far too many questions. I pulled out my phone and opened the picture of Jason I had saved from the yearbook. Dark skin, giant afro, brown eyes, a kind smile, football jersey. I could see the resemblance between us.

"Are you sure you want to do this right now?" I locked my phone and scooted my desk chair closer to her. Her eyes flashed up at me.

"I told you I'm fine. This is what I need right now."

I mouthed "okay" as I turned back around. It had been ten days since the funeral, and it seemed like Jason Pritchard was officially a ghost. Every single lead we came across was a dead end. It was like he had disappeared off the face of the planet.

"What if we went to the P.O. Box and asked around?" Mela sounded hopeful.

"I'm grounded, Mel, remember?" I wasn't sure how much longer the grounding was going to last. It had been almost two months, and it was borderline imprisonment as far as I was concerned. By the look on Mela's face, she agreed.

"Let me take care of it. This is ridiculous." She was up and out of my room before I could open my mouth.

Fifteen minutes later she waltzed back in, triumphantly holding her car keys and grabbing her purse. Whatever she said to my parents had sprung me from my cell, and I wasn't about to ask questions until we were safely out of the house.

Just as we were about to leave, my dad called my name from the living room.

"Save yourself!" I whispered, and shoved Mela out the door dramatically as she shook with laughter all the way to her car.

"Yes, Dad?" I stood in the doorframe of the living room waiting for a speech, judging by the look on his face. He took a deep breath before he spoke.

"You really hurt your mother by looking for your birth father.

We supported you last year when you wanted to meet Ali, but this is different. You don't know this man at all, and he could be dangerous. Please stop this foolishness. You're not grounded anymore—but, Olivia, so help me if I find out you've been looking for him again. Promise me you won't start the search back up."

The lines on his face seemed to have deepened since the last time we had really spoken. His mouth was tight, and he looked exhausted.

"Dad, I promise I won't start the search again."

He nodded and waved me off.

It wasn't technically a lie. I had never stopped the search, after all.

We stopped at Nate's, and the four of us hopped into Lucas's truck to take the seventy-five-minute drive to the town where Jason's P.O. Box was. It was a long shot, and I might not have even bothered, but since my freedoms had been revoked for several weeks, I would have gone on a road trip to Chick-fil-A at that point.

Armed with iced coffees and Mela's playlist, we headed South on the I-95. Take two on finding my family, courtesy of my friends. I drank a long sip of my coffee and smiled at Lucas.

"Freedom tastes good?"

"Freedom tastes incredible." I grinned as Nate and Mela laughed from the backseat.

"So, what's it like being grounded? Is it like prison? Do you get your meals left on a tray outside your door?" Nate asked.

I turned in my seat to gawk at him.

"I'm sorry, what? You've never been grounded?" I made myself close my mouth, but my eyes were still wide.

"Uh, no. My parents don't believe in that kind of parenting." He shrugged as I went back to gaping at him.

"Wow. Can I move in with you too?"

Mela slapped my shoulder good naturedly. "Get in line." I saw the faint blush that had just colored Nate's cheeks. Nate reached for her hand and gave her a look that made me feel like I was intruding on something.

They made me smile, but my joy was short lived. When we pulled into the town, my stomach churned. It looked like it might have been a nice place at one point, but now it was decrepit and had an ominous feel to it. Many of the businesses along the main strip—if you could call it that—were boarded up and abandoned. The sidewalks hadn't been maintained, and large cracks ran through the length of them. Lucas slowed the truck to look for the post office, and the few people who were out stopped and openly stared at the truck as though they knew we were outsiders who didn't belong there.

"This place gives me the creeps," Mela muttered as though she was worried someone outside would hear her.

"It's not so bad," I found myself saying out loud. It was horrible, but I felt like I needed to defend the place since my birth father had at least had a mailbox there. Lucas shot me a doubtful look. I pursed my lips, refusing to agree with them.

We pulled into the post office parking lot, and it was every bit as rundown as most of the businesses in the town.

"It's like we stepped back in time." Nate looked around with his mouth hanging open.

"Okay, okay. Let's just get this over with." I hopped out of the truck with the rest of them in tow.

A bell rang as I opened the door to the post office, and the sound jolted the employee out of his sleep. He looked genuinely confused as to his whereabouts for a solid minute and finally turned to look at the four of us, who stood frozen just inside the door.

"Well, *you're* not from around here." The way he sucked his teeth made my skin crawl. He couldn't have been more than twenty, and between his greasy, black, scaly hair and the way he undressed both Mela and me with his eyes—somehow simultaneously—I wanted to throw up. Mela squeezed my hand tightly three times—our code for when a guy was creeping one of us out and we wanted to leave.

"We're looking for information on someone who rented P.O. Box 947 about seventeen years ago."

Nate's voice caught me off guard, but he had stepped forward and was the one asking questions. He turned around and winked at the two of us before turning back and waiting for the guy's answer. I felt Mela relax beside me.

"Seventeen years ago? Good luck, buddy. Besides, I can't give out that information. It's confidential." He tried to peer around Nate to look at us again, but Nate was blocking Mela completely. Lucas, the taller of the two, stepped up to the counter.

"Look, we came a long way to get this information, so the least you could do is look it up in your system."

"And, uh, why would I do that?" McGreasy sat back in his chair and folded his arms behind his head.

I couldn't see the look on Lucas' face but by the way McGreasy's creepy grin faded and he sprang into action immediately, I was kind of glad. I caught Mela's eye, and she gave me a *no one messes with your man* kind of look that made me grin. McGreasy kept typing, and beads of sweat were beginning to form on his forehead.

"Our records only go back ten years. I swear." He put his hands up defensively.

"Who had it ten years ago?" I asked.

He squinted at the computer screen. "Seth Horrowitz. Is that it?" He was speaking to Lucas and very deliberately not looking at anyone else.

Lucas nodded, and we headed back out to the truck. Even though I had known it would be a dead end, I was still disappointed. *What if he's dead?* I squeezed my own shoulder to try and release the tension that had built up. How could one person be so hard to find? He wasn't on social media, didn't exist on Google—beyond going to South Fork High School, it was like he just didn't exist. An idea was brewing, but I didn't know how or if it would pan out.

"Wouldn't the high school have the address he lived at when he attended there?" I asked. "He couldn't have given a P.O. Box as his address. He would have had to prove that he lived in the district. Right?" I held my breath. Maybe it was a stupid idea.

"You're a genius, Liv!" Mela slapped me from the back.

"Well, it's not like they're going to just give us that information," I mumbled.

"Not a bunch of high school kids, no." I knew that tone. I turned to look at her, and she pumped her eyebrows and pulled out her phone.

"What are you—" She shushed me as her phone started ringing.

"South Fork High School." I immediately imagined a heavy-set woman with square glasses and a permanent grimace on the other side.

"This is Detective Kepper with the Broward County Sheriff Department. I'm looking for some information on a suspect who is currently at large." Mela had adopted a much more sophisticated voice in a matter of seconds. We all stared at her, both horrified and impressed.

"Who is it?" The lady on the phone didn't sound all that surprised. Was this a regular occurrence at that school?

"Jason Pritchard. He would have attended quite a while ago." Mela shrugged at me, glad it was working.

"Please hold." We all held our breath. After two minutes she came back on the line. *"322 Queen St., White City."*

"Thank you, ma'am." Mela was struggling to maintain her composure.

"I don't know how much help that's going to be, though." The woman's voice was flat.

"Why is that?"

"Because it's a foster home. Only kids who are bounced around the system get placed there until they age out."

"You're saying Jason Pritchard was in foster care?" Mela sounded like her seventeen-year-old self again, having forgotten her persona.

"That's what I'm saying. Have a nice day."

The unmistakable click of the phone might as well have been a gunshot. The silence among us was deafening.

16

I watched the trees whiz by in a blur as we headed to White City. It was another thirty minutes farther south, and the drive home would be nearly two hours. None of us seemed to care. It hadn't even been a conversation. Lucas had simply put the address in his phone, and we'd taken off. I stared out the window, imagining Jason growing up in foster care. I had just assumed he'd grown up in a family, like Ali did. *Maybe it wasn't so bad,* I tried to convince myself. There were good foster homes, weren't there?

Lucas squeezed my hand tightly without looking over at me, as though he knew I would need time to digest the news. It was late afternoon when we pulled up to the house. It seemed nice enough. There was a tire swing hanging from a large tree in the front yard and the walkway up to the house was done with interlock pavers, though weeds had grown through in many places. The grass had several burnt patches on it but otherwise was relatively green. The garden in front of the house didn't seem to have been tended to lately, but it might have been nice once, with a few flowers still doing their best to reach the sun.

The four of us sat in the truck, and I could feel the weight of the responsibility of this knowledge.

"Liv?"

I flinched at the sound of Lucas's voice.

You don't know this man at all, he could be dangerous. My dad's words replayed in my mind like a child taunting a schoolmate on the playground.

"Just because he was in foster care doesn't mean anything," I said, answering them both.

"No one said he was some kind of screw up—" Mela said.

"But you're all thinking it." I accused them with my own fears like a coward.

No one said anything else, and we walked up to the door at the slow crawl of a funeral procession. The door knocker was rusted out and the green paint, once vibrant, was faded and missing altogether in some places. I took a deep breath and rapped my knuckle against the door three times.

The door swung open and standing before us was a toddler in a fragrant diaper and nothing else. His blue eyes were red, and his face tearstained as he stared at us.

"Jimmy! Close the door."

I started. The sound came from a woman whose raspy voice might have been acquired by smoking a pack of cigarettes a day for the last forty years.

Peering around the door, I saw three more children, maybe seven or eight years old, running through the house and chucking things at each other. Though the sun was still in the sky, the room behind the door was dark, with the curtains pulled tightly closed. The television was playing an episode of *The Young and the Restless,* and there were piles of clothing on the floor.

My eyes widened as I took in the scene and looked to see that Lucas, Mela, and Nate were all mirroring my reaction. *Doesn't mean anything. I'm sure it's a good home.*

"Hello?" I called out with trepidation.

The woman swore under her breath and heaved herself out

of whatever she had been sitting on. She showed up in the doorway with a lit cigarette hanging from her mouth, wearing a large, stained Mumu dress. Her hair was a mix of blond and gray and was thin and straggly.

"Can I help you?" she asked warily as she took a puff of her cigarette, inhaled and exhaled, all without removing it from her lips.

This can't be where he lived. Maybe she wasn't in charge then.

"I'm looking for information about one of your former foster children. Although it was a long time ago so maybe it was before your time?" My voice was shaky.

Her eyes narrowed. "It's been me and my husband running this home for forty years. You're not even supposed to have this address." She looked me up and down.

"I'm sorry." I cleared my throat as I felt my neck and face flush. Who else was going to accuse me of trespassing this year? "This is important, though."

"Who are you looking for and why?" she demanded and blew out another breath of smoke above my head.

"Jason Pritchard. He's my birth father, and I'd like to find him." I decided that honesty was probably the best course of action. I held my breath, hoping she wouldn't slam the door in my face.

"Well, come in then." She sounded resigned as she waddled back into the house and left the door open for us to follow her.

I turned around and stopped the three of them from following me.

"I need to do this on my own," I whispered.

Each of them opened their mouths to object, but I didn't give them time to speak and quickly closed the door behind me. Whatever she was about to disclose, I felt the need to protect Jason from anyone other than me bearing witness to it.

"Breanna, change Jimmy's diaper," the scraggly-haired woman barked to someone I couldn't see.

A girl who couldn't have been older than eleven came into the room and sighed as she picked up the toddler and carried him off as though she had done it a thousand times before.

"All right, what was his name again?" She was using the end of her cigarette to light another one.

"Jason Pritchard." I held back a cough, not wanting to set her off. I had a feeling she spooked easily.

"Karl!"

I jerked as I stood in the middle of the room. I hadn't been invited to sit down and I wasn't about to make myself comfortable.

An older man with gray hair, sagging skin, and a turned-down mouth that seemed set that way walked into the room at a snail's pace. He was wearing a plaid sweater and dirty jeans, and he balked at my presence, narrowing his eyes suspiciously.

"What?" He sounded gruff and uninviting.

"Do you remember a Jason Pritchard? She's looking for her daddy." Her mocking tone was met with a sneer by him.

"Are we supposed to be remembering the names of all of these…children?" The way he said *children* made me think he really meant delinquents.

"I think it might have been somewhere between eighteen and twenty years ago if that helps. It sounds like he was aging out of the system," I said to move things along. My eyes were burning from the smoke.

He stepped toward me and leaned in so closely that I backed right into a shelf with ratty-looking books on it. I drew myself up and he raised his eyebrows in response.

"Jason…" He stroked his chin thoughtfully. I saw clarity brighten his dull eyes. "Wasn't he the one whose aunt dropped him off when he was five but kept his siblings?"

My heart dropped into my stomach. *No, please, don't let that be his story.*

"You know, I think you might be right, Karl." She was lighting another cigarette.

"He was *here* from five to eighteen?" I blurted it out without meaning to.

"Here? Lord, no. He was bounced around from home to home for most of those years. He finished here, though—had nowhere else to go by then. Did his time and got the hell out."

Karl had plopped down on the couch beside what must be his wife as she spoke. I wasn't sure which scenario would have been worse—staying here the whole time or bouncing around.

"Do you know where he moved to after he left?" I was pinching the bridge of my nose to block out the smoke and the knowledge that these people didn't seem to care about the kids who came through their house.

"No. We don't keep tabs on them once they leave." Karl was busy choosing something to watch. *Once the paycheck leaves, more like it.*

"Katrina, what did I say about throwing things in the house?"

The woman's angry words reverberated through my mind, making my headache even worse. It was time to leave.

"Okay, well, thanks anyway." I moved toward the door. They hadn't even bothered to stand up. I shook my head and opened the door to leave.

"I saw him in Aberdeen once. Might try there." This came from Karl, who was still clicking through the channels. I was shocked that he had actually given me anything to go on.

"Thanks. I'll do that."

He harumphed in response and I closed the door behind me.

My eyes pooled with tears that I quickly blinked away. I took a deep breath to stuff down my emotions. Now was not the time to fall apart.

As soon as I got back in the truck, Mela wanted answers that I couldn't give her.

"Liv, what did they say?" she asked.

"I just want to go home please."

My eyes pleaded with Lucas, and he nodded his understanding as he started the truck. There would be time to tell them what happened, but that time was not right now. They dropped me off at home and I squeezed Mela's hand before I jumped out. I would keep my promise to Renae, but I just needed some space to fall apart on my own first.

17

I stuffed another soaked tissue into my right pocket and pulled a fresh one out of my left one. Tears streamed down my face as I looked out at the water from the rocks at Hillsboro Beach. The sea was gray and violent, and the white caps from the waves breaking seemed to be trying to claim one of the birds soaring above.

Visions assaulted my mind of a small, terrified boy knocking on the door of that foster home. Separated from his siblings and relinquished by his aunt. I couldn't quite comprehend the level of fear, of heartbreak, of emotional damage that would have caused him.

The roar of the ocean waves masked the sound of Lucas's feet on the rocks behind me, so his hand on my shoulder made me jump. He sat down beside me wordlessly and I didn't offer any explanation for my tears. After several minutes, I finally broke the silence.

"I don't see how my birth father could possibly be okay. The life he's lived. The pain he must have endured. I'm just not sure what we'll find if we find him. He would have every right to be in jail or worse." I rested my forehead on my knees and let the tears continue to fall on the rocks below me.

Lucas simply sat holding space for me. He stayed quiet while I cried for the little boy dropped off at a strange house without a familiar face in sight. It was almost too much for my heart to take. How could Ali have known that he grew up in foster care and still refused to let him keep me?

"I still believe that you could be the one to save him, Liv. But if you want to call the whole thing off, just say the word. We'll be at Nate's when you're ready." He squeezed my arm and stood up to leave.

I grabbed his hand, and he gave me a questioning look.

"Do you really think so?"

"I do."

I nodded and continued to hold his hand, gathering the strength I needed to stand up.

"Then let's go to Aberdeen."

"LET'S TRY THE BAKERY." Mela was in her element, showing Jason's yearbook picture to different businesses to see if they recognized him.

It was Saturday, and the four of us were walking through the quaint little town of Aberdeen. We had tried the grocery store, the post office, and a Starbucks so far but with no luck. Mela practically danced up the steps to the bakery, dragging Nate along with her. It was the happiest I had seen her since her mom died. She always did love a good mystery to solve.

Lucas and I shared a smile. I was trying not to get my hopes up; I knew it was a long shot. Just because Karl had seen Jason one time in this town didn't mean that he had set roots down and lived here now. He could be anywhere. But I found myself hopeful despite it all.

"Do you happen to know this man?" Mela was showing the picture to a pimply-faced teenager.

"I don't think so. Let me ask my manager though. He knows almost everyone in town."

He walked to the back and returned in a minute accompanied by an older gentleman with a beard so long he resembled some kind of wizard.

"Let me take a look at the picture."

He seemed as eager as Mela. By the looks of the small town, this might have been the most interesting thing to have happened in years. He put his spectacles on and took the phone from Mela to get a closer look.

"He looks familiar, but I can't be sure."

"Well, the picture is almost twenty years old," Mela said hopefully.

"Hmmm, in that case he does look like someone who comes in here a couple times a month. I think his name is Johnny, or Jimmy…"

"Jason, maybe?" My heart was in my throat.

"That might be it. Very nice man," he murmured thoughtfully as he stroked his beard.

"Do you know when he was in last?"

"I think he came in last week for some Danishes. This is a very popular spot, you know." He winked with all the pride of a small-town bakery owner.

"In that case, we'll take four butter tarts please." Nate looked over and winked at me, reminding me of running into each other at Le Petit Pain several weeks ago when I was buying butter tarts for my parents—trying to be a better daughter.

Instantly I felt the sting of guilt, knowing that my parents would be upset that I was still looking for Jason. I wished they could understand I could no sooner give up this search than I could stop breathing. There was a need beyond my comprehension pulling me forward, no matter how many dead ends we ran into. I just knew that finding him would…fix me.

We headed to a park in the middle of the town to sit on the grass and eat our butter tarts. I leaned against a palm tree and savored every bite. It was a busy day, with elderly couples strolling down the walking path, parents pushing their little ones on the swings, and families enjoying picnics on the grass. People took notice of us, but unlike at White City, they smiled and nodded instead of openly staring. This town definitely had a friendlier, cozier vibe.

"So where to next?" Mela's eyes were bright with excitement and likely a sugar rush. "I have a good feeling about this place."

"I mean, the bakery owner wasn't completely sure it was him." I was trying to bring Mela back down to earth a little. Her enthusiasm was so high I was beginning to worry what the disappointment might do to her if we didn't find him. She had channeled all her grief into this search, perhaps feeling that she could end my pain even if she couldn't stop her own—and I didn't want to think of what disappointment might do to her.

"He was pretty sure it was." Mela's steady gaze was challenging me.

I threw my hands up. "It's possible, I guess." The truth was that the closer we came to finding him, the more nervous I was about what we would find. I felt like I needed more time to process things, but I was running out of it.

"Why don't we go to the diner up the street? I'm starving." Nate rubbed his stomach, making us laugh.

"Dude, you just ate a butter tart." Lucas punched him playfully in the shoulder.

"That was like one bite." Nate looked thoroughly offended that we could expect his stomach to be satisfied with a single tart.

Lucas pulled me to my feet and we headed to the diner together. It was called the Milk and Honey Diner and was exactly what one would expect to find in a small town in America. Red leather booths, a mini jukebox at every table, pictures of famous singers who had visited the diner and signed a framed picture proudly displayed for all to see, and the smell of greasy food wafting through the restaurant. The smells made my mouth water, and I was suddenly famished. We got seated quickly and placed our drink orders with the hostess while we waited for our server and looked over the menu. I couldn't decide between a burger and fries, or a chicken Caesar wrap with onion rings. Decisions, decisions. Even deciding what was for lunch proved a challenge.

In the end, we split a platter of frings, a combination of fries and onion rings, Nate got a triple burger, Mela ordered a cheeseburger, Lucas got a regular burger, and I got the wrap knowing that he would give me bites of his burger. We discussed more places to try while we ate.

"There was a pharmacy a block away and some unique shops along Main Street. I say we try them all," Mela said with her mouth full.

"Babe." Nate was looking at her with a French fry halfway to his mouth.

"Sorry, this is so good." She took another bite of her cheeseburger as she said it, and we all laughed.

Each time the waitress came to check on us, Mela's mouth was too full to allow her to ask if the girl recognized Jason. The rest of us were really enjoying the poorly timed entrances, and Mela's annoyance and inability to chew fast enough to ask her.

"Ugh, that's it. I'm not taking another bite until she comes back." She huffed impatiently.

I snickered as I watched the waitress approach nearly every other booth to check on the customers before noticing Mela's desperation and coming back to us. I was almost sorry the entertainment was over, or maybe I was only still delaying the inevitable.

"Sorry, guys, is everything okay?" She looked worried, no doubt assessing how much of a tip she was likely to get.

"Yes, the food is incredible. I just have a question for you."

Mela had piqued her curiosity. "Okay…" She glanced at me as though hoping for an explanation. I shrugged in response.

Mela held up the phone to her with the picture of Jason on it. "Have you seen him before? The picture is old, but—"

The waitress leaned in to get a closer look and surprise registered on her face. "Oh my gosh, yeah, that's Jason Pritchard! I know him, great guy. Ha! Is that his yearbook picture?" She laughed.

My mouth was dry, and Mela gaped at her.

"Do you know if he's from around here?" Lucas asked the question carefully, as though defusing a bomb.

"Mmmhmm, he comes in here almost every morning. He lives on Firefly Court, just a few minutes from here."

The only things I could hear were the ringing in my ears and the gasp that escaped my lips. *We've actually found him.*

18

"I can't do this, you guys."

We were sitting in the truck in front of 321 Firefly Court, where we had been for the last twenty minutes.

The front door of the house was buttercream yellow with a wreath hanging from it. A vertical "welcome" sign rested against the wall. The porch had two rocking chairs off to the side, and a string of outdoor lights hung from the ceiling and wrapped around the railing. A cobblestone pathway led up to the porch, and a cute garden had been planted below the window. It all seemed well cared for, which didn't account for the sinking feeling in the pit of my stomach.

"Maybe it would help if you told us what's stopping you?" Mela was trying to sound sympathetic, but I heard the frustration in her voice.

I couldn't blame her. I'd been waiting for this moment for a year and here I was, sitting outside of his house, and I couldn't bring myself to get out of the truck. What was I going to say? *Hi, I'm your daughter?* It felt so...abrupt. In all the time I'd spent searching, I hadn't planned what I would do if I actually found him. Now I was sitting outside of his house like a stalker, and I wasn't sure whether I was going to make myself walk up to his door or not.

"I don't know what to say to him." It felt so foolish to say it out loud, but I had made the three of them sit here with no explanation for twenty minutes. I had to give them something. The truth was that there was a sense of doom hanging over my head, and no matter how hard I tried to shake it off, I couldn't seem to get rid of it.

"Aww, Liv, he's going to be so happy to meet you." This time it was Nate trying to sound sympathetic.

"You don't know that." What if it was another Ali situation? I didn't think I could handle that heartbreak. Maybe it was enough just to know that he was alive and seemed like a nice man from what people had said. Not to mention the fact that the anxiety in my chest was beginning to cause me physical pain.

"Do you want me to talk to him first?" Lucas offered.

I immediately wanted to reject his offer, but as I thought about it, the idea seemed pretty reasonable. Lucas could go up to the door and make sure it was really him, and then if he seemed unhappy about us being there, we could just leave. Even as I had the thought, I knew I couldn't say yes. This was something I needed to do.

"No. I mean, I do want you to do it, don't get me wrong, but I think I need to be the one to talk to him first. But…not alone this time. Will you guys come with me?" I sounded timid as I tried to muster as much courage as I could. They all agreed.

"I had no intention of letting you leave me out of this," Mela remarked snidely. I threw her a grateful glance.

"Okay, guys, let's do this before I chicken out again."

As soon as we hopped out of the truck, Lucas locked the doors and I couldn't help but feel as though it was on purpose, so I didn't have a place to escape to. His wide grin confirmed my suspicions.

"You've got this."

He kissed my forehead and held out his hand like the lifeline it was. I took it gratefully as Nate and Mela trailed behind us. One foot in front of the other on the cobblestone path. I was walking so awkwardly that I was sure I resembled a bride walking down the aisle. Right foot forward, left together. Left foot forward, right together. I must have looked ridiculous, but no one said anything, probably knowing that at any moment I could start running in the opposite direction. Every step closer to the door made the sense of foreboding within me get stronger.

Too soon I was on the porch, with nothing else to do but knock. My hand was shaking so badly that I pulled it back to hide it. Lucas looked at me, seeking permission to knock as he jerked his head toward the door. I nodded my agreement and felt the four of us hold our breath as Lucas knocked three times.

Less than a minute later the door opened and a girl with dark skin, who looked a couple of years younger than me, stood there. She was in overalls and a white crop top and had long hair braided down her back. Was she family? My sister maybe? *I hope not.* My eyebrows rose at my inner dialogue.

"Can I help you?" she asked.

"Umm, does Jason Pritchard live here?" I didn't sound like myself at all, but I was proud that I got the words out at least.

"Yes…who are you?" Her forehead creased in confusion as she looked the four of us up and down.

"My name is Olivia, and these are my friends." It was all I could think to say. I wasn't about to let this stranger introduce me to Jason as his daughter. Who was she even? I had assumed he'd be living alone.

"Okay—uh, come in, I guess." She stepped aside. "Uncle Jase, some people are here to see you!" she called out across the house as we stood in the doorway.

Uncle! A sense of relief I didn't understand flooded through me.

Jason came around the corner and my heart jumped into my throat. He looked just like his yearbook picture minus the giant afro, with some extra padding around the middle, and the fact that his face had aged some. He was in cargo shorts and a black t-shirt.

"Hello...?" He gave us a quizzical look, and I immediately felt disappointed that he didn't recognize me.

"Hi..." I squeaked out, then cleared my throat and tried to speak again. "I'm Olivia. You would probably know me as Rose Schafer, though..." The idea to introduce myself with the name they had given me originally had just come to me, and I was grateful for it. It felt much less in your face than "Hey, I'm your kid."

It did the trick. His eyes widened as he took in my appearance and searched my face—for what I didn't know, but he seemed to find what he was looking for and needed to lean on a side table until he regained his composure.

"Wow," he whispered. "I didn't think I would ever see you again."

He took a few steps forward and pulled me into a bear hug. I stiffened at the closeness of this stranger and immediately chided myself. *You finally find him, he's happy to see you, and you feel awkward that he's hugging you? Get it together, Liv.* He smelled like aftershave and soap. After what felt like the longest minute of my life, I pulled back and he let me go. Mela was wiping a tear from her eye and the guys were smiling.

"Not to break up the party, but...who is this, Uncle Jase?" The girl didn't sound annoyed, just genuinely baffled.

"Right! I guess you wouldn't know. Kimmie, this is my daughter." He looked...proud.

"Your *daughter*? I didn't know you had a kid."

My heart sank a little. He hadn't told her about me. Maybe it was just her. Maybe she was too young or something. We were still awkwardly standing in his doorway.

"Yeah, sorry. Sometimes you bury things in your heart so deeply that only *you* know about them. This is one of those times. Come in, come in." He gestured for us to follow him into the house. "Don't worry about your shoes." He threw in as I was about to take mine off.

We walked into a quaint living room with a black couch and matching loveseat and chairs. There was a red and white patterned rug on the floor, a wall unit with an impressive collection of DVDs, and a large window that flooded the room with sunlight. The room opened up into a beautiful kitchen, complete with marble backsplash and countertops. The four of us took a seat on the couch together as Jason asked us what we wanted to drink and went on to the kitchen.

"You good?" Mela whispered into my ear.

"Yeah. Why?" I whispered back.

"Because your face looks like you're being held at gunpoint."

I grimaced as I realized the smile I had plastered on my face wasn't fooling anyone. My heart was still in my throat, and I kept replaying Jason's words in my mind. *Sometimes you bury things in your heart so deeply that only you know about them.* Neither of my birth parents had told anyone about me. What was so wrong with me that my own blood relatives didn't want anyone to know I existed?

Jason came back with a pitcher of iced tea and poured a glass for each of us, then dropped into the loveseat next to his niece.

"Okay, so I know you, Olivia, and this is my niece Kimmie. Who are your friends?" His smile was friendly, easygoing.

"This is my best friend Mela, her boyfriend Nate, and this is my boyfriend Lucas." I wasn't sure why I gave everyone a title, but it was too late to take it back.

"Really nice to meet all of you."

My mouth was dry, but my hands were shaking so badly that I didn't dare try to take a sip of my iced tea.

"You have a lovely home." It was terrible and boring, but I couldn't think of anything else to say.

"Oh, thank you. It's actually not my home, though. I just rent a room here, but the owner is fantastic."

He and Kimmie exchanged a wink and a laugh at their inside

joke, and I felt a pang of jealousy at the sight. I wriggled in my seat and sank farther into the oversized cushion.

"So, Olivia, tell me about yourself. I want to know everything." He sat forward in his seat expectantly and I froze.

"Uh…" I felt my face flush as I suddenly couldn't remember a single detail about my life.

"She's an amazing athlete." Lucas came to my rescue, and I blew my breath out with relief.

"Yeah? What's your sport?" I met his eyes—kind, brown, twinkly.

"Track." It came out so low that I had to repeat it a little louder.

"Nice! I played football in high school and loved it."

"Lucas and Nate play football," I said, my tone flat.

The three of them spent the next fifteen minutes talking football, and I was grateful for every minute of it. I had spent so long wishing for this moment, and it was all wrong. It felt so uncomfortable.

After a few minutes, he turned to me and asked the million-dollar question.

"How did you guys find me?"

My palms got sweaty right away. I knew he would ask eventually, and I hated that I would have to tell him what I knew. I swallowed hard before answering him.

"It took a while. I registered my name on the adoption registry, but we weren't matched, so that was a dead end." I coughed to buy myself some time. I desperately wanted to ask him why he hadn't registered, but I couldn't bring myself to do it.

"Ah, yes, I never did register my name on that thing. I figured if it was meant to be, then you'd find your way back to me. And you did." His eyes brimmed with emotion.

He never looked for me. I forced myself to compartmentalize that piece of information until I could deal with it.

"After a bit of running around, we ended up at your old

foster home in White City. Karl mentioned that he had seen you in this town once, so we came to check it out—and our waitress told us where we could find you. I hope that was okay…" I trailed off. I hadn't meant to give him so many details but once I started, I felt like I had to explain it all.

His eyes had narrowed when I mentioned Karl, but otherwise he listened politely.

"Yeah, things got pretty dark after leaving that foster home. It was the last one I was at before aging out of the system. Once you turn eighteen, they cut you loose. After I relinquished my parental rights to you, I really hit rock bottom. I was drinking all the time and was so far into depression that I ended up homeless for a while."

I wanted to cry listening to him tell us his story. Homeless or incarcerated had been the two fates I had been most worried about for him. My heartbreak was magnified by the knowledge that he hadn't bothered to look for me; I had just assumed he would have at least tried. But maybe he had just pulled his life together. I had to give him a chance to explain, but a pain was growing in my chest that made it hard for me to take deep breaths. Again, I forced myself to go on.

"You seem to have picked your life back up. How?" I tried to sound casual, but I was burning to know how he'd done it. Homeless to stable seemed like a big leap, and I needed to know who had saved him if it wasn't me.

"I had bigger priorities than my own demons I suppose." He grabbed Kimmie's hand affectionately and gazed at her with an expression that made me suddenly want to throw up. "When she was born, I knew that I would need to get my life together if I was going to be in hers. Sometimes there are reasons beyond yourself that cause you to grow up and you pick yourself back up, not because you want to, but because you have to." He beamed at her, and she smiled back at him as though she'd heard the story a million times before.

Mela squeezed my hand intuitively while I fought for

composure. I hated her. I hated her with a hatred I had never known I could feel. I wanted to reach across the room and choke her. I squeezed my hands tightly together just in case they decided to act on their own. It felt like I was losing control of myself.

Mela yelped, and I realized I was breaking her bones while trying to break my own. I loosened the grip and she slipped her fingers out, shaking them.

"That's wonderful," I managed to say. "I'm so happy for you."

My voice was strong and confident though I felt all the opposite, but my walls had gone up. It was as though my brain was protecting me from processing what I had just heard. I hadn't been the one to save him. Not by a long shot. It didn't really seem like he had even given me a second thought. Once again, I was not important enough to fight for.

"Let me get you guys a snack." Jason stood up and Kimmie followed him.

I watched the two of them laughing together in the kitchen. I envied the ease of their relationship. He moved in synchronicity with her, as though they'd been doing this dance forever whereas I felt like an ostrich trying to fly. I didn't belong here. And if I didn't belong with either of my birth parents, then where *did* I belong?

Nowhere, kiddo.

"We should get going." I stood up, knowing that I had about three minutes before I broke down—and I sure as hell wasn't about to do that here.

I could feel everyone staring at me as though I had just grown a second head.

"Sorry, I just remembered that there is a mandatory track practice tonight and I'm already on thin ice, so I really can't miss it." It was a ten out of ten on the terrible-excuse scale, but I figured no one was going to argue with me, and I was right.

"Oh, that's too bad." Jason looked at me sympathetically, and I smiled.

"It's okay. I'm sure we'll meet again." I didn't mean to sound so formal, but the last thing I wanted at that second was to see him again.

"Well, let me give you my number at least." He bent down to write it on a piece of paper and handed it to me before hugging me again.

I hugged him back stiffly, the way I would placate a distant relative. The air was getting thin, and stars were beginning to dance around my eyes as I pulled away.

"It was nice to meet you, Jason." I nodded awkwardly as Mela, Nate, and Lucas waited for me beyond the open front door.

"It was a dream come true, baby girl," he said.

Right. A dream you did absolutely nothing to make happen.

"See ya."

I walked out and right by my friends. I wanted to scream at the top of my lungs or cry or punch something, but I would settle for a silent drive away from yet another parent who had discarded me and never looked back.

19

Deep breath in through the nose, exhale through the mouth. Left arm up, right leg up. Right arm up, left leg up. Switch, switch, switch, faster and faster and faster until my lungs burned and demanded air in that achingly painful and familiar way. Sweat cascaded into my eyes and my ponytail swung from side to side as I continued sprinting down the beach.

I glanced at the water and the sun blinded me, making a memory flash in my mind of Jason smiling at Kimmie with all the affection of a doting father. My breath caught and messed up my rhythm, and it forced me to slow down before starting over. My watch indicated it was almost time for me to meet with Lucas. I got back to the parking lot just as he was pulling in. He was in shorts and a white tank top, and I tried not to stare as he walked over to me.

"Hey, I'm glad you called. I've been worried." He pulled me into a hug and I let him, but I didn't hug him back.

"I'm fine," I repeated for what felt like the millionth time over the last twenty-four hours. "I'm fine" to Mela, "I'm fine" to my parents, "I'm fine" to myself. *I'm fine.*

"You're not fine, Liv. Give me a break. You didn't say a word the entire drive home yesterday." He folded his arms and stared at me.

"I don't need to talk about what happened, okay?" I gave him a warning look and hoped that he would drop it.

"Liv—"

My hand rose automatically to stop him from what I knew he was about to say.

"It's not a big deal."

"I saw the look on your face," he countered immediately, daring me to argue with him.

I winced, imagining what I had looked like during the visit with Jason. What I had looked like watching my birth father dote on his niece and only tolerate me. Even now I wanted to cringe, knowing that Lucas had witnessed the whole thing. Of course, he had; he had pushed me into it.

"I don't think you want to insist on this, Lucas."

He raised his eyebrows. "And why is that?"

"None of this would have happened if you hadn't pushed me into it. I focused on finding Jason because *you* said that I could be the one to save him." He flinched at my accusatory tone. "I convinced myself that he must have had a good reason not to register. That he was looking for me in some other capacity. But he wasn't, and I could have lived blissfully unaware of that fact if *you* hadn't convinced me to keep going." I hated that my voice cracked.

"Liv—" He reached for me.

"Don't!" I stepped away. "Finding him was supposed to complete me. He was supposed to make me feel whole. But instead…instead I'm more screwed up than ever."

Lucas had stopped trying to hold me. "Don't I count for anything?"

"You don't get it. *Your* dad came looking for you. *You* grew up with your mom. I should have never listened to you when you told me to keep looking for him. 'Maybe you'll be the one to save him.'" I put my fingers up in air quotes and rolled my eyes.

He scoffed. "I should have known you'd do this."

"What exactly am I doing?" The words were bitter. More than I had intended.

"You push people away and then complain when they're not there."

The lump in my throat was suffocating me. I turned away from him so that he wouldn't see me trying, and failing, to compose myself. I was tired of appearing weak around Lucas.

"But he's happy to have met you, Liv," Lucas went on. "He said that he hit rock bottom when he lost you, right? He wants to be in your life. You're just going to throw that away because it didn't happen the way you wanted it to?"

I stiffened at his words.

"I think I know when I'm not wanted, Lucas. You couldn't possibly understand."

It was his time to roll his eyes at me. "Would you stop? You think I've had some perfect life? Look, I know you wanted to be the one to save him, but you weren't. You need to get over it. You've been so obsessed by the idea of saving him you're actually pissed he's okay."

"How dare you?"

"It's true, and you know it. I knew it the second you saw he wasn't living in some hellhole. It disappointed you, Liv. Just admit it." His green eyes flashed with anger as he studied my face.

I felt sick. Was that why I had a sinking feeling, sitting outside Jason's house? But there was no time for me to process that possibility. Fighting with anyone too often felt like I was fighting for my life, and I needed to be on the attack.

"If I'm such a monster, why are you even with me?" I demanded.

Lucas' eyes softened and he reached for me, but I pulled away. Pain flashed across his face.

"Because I love you." His voice was soft, and he faltered on the last word. He had never told me he loved me before. Why would he choose this moment?

"You don't know what you're saying." I shook my head like he was nuts. This was all wrong. He didn't love me. How could he?

"That's all you have to say?" He looked incredulous.

"What do you want from me? You need to stop trying to fix what's broken. People can't save each other." I turned away and walked toward the water.

"You're so damn selfish, Liv."

I whipped back around with my fists clenched. "Selfish? How do you figure?"

"You'll never let anyone get too close, will you? Nothing will ever fill the void in your heart. You're determined to do life on your own, be the hero and the villain of your story. There's no room for anyone else, is there?" He glared back at me.

"This coming from someone who just claimed to love me. Lucas, you don't love me. You just want to save me because you couldn't save your mom. So blinded by your ambition to protect her, you can't even see who I really am. You think you love me, but you don't even know me."

No one does.

He flinched again as though I had slapped him across the face, and I didn't apologize.

Though we were mere feet from each other, the words we couldn't take back had built a palisade around us. We had made sharp stakes and planted them facing each other. Don't come any nearer. I've got the weapons to destroy you.

Maybe he wasn't thinking the same way; he trained his eyes on me like I was a wild animal he needed to be leery of. I searched his face, but I couldn't see past the verbal darts he had hurled at me. The ocean might as well have been between us instead of beside us. Maybe it was for the best. Where could this have gone, really? Two broken people didn't make a whole one.

And this was the feeling I could not shake: It was only a matter of time until he threw me away too. Might as well beat him to the punch.

As the sting of our words hung in the air, I did the one thing I knew without a doubt was embedded into my DNA: I walked away. And for the very first time, he let me.

20

"Go!" Coach Addison clapped his hands together and the eight of us took off around the bend of the track.

The 400-meter race was brutal, and I leaned into every bit of the pain. I was in lane one, which meant I had to start behind everyone, but I could also surprise people that way. They tended to write off the first lane, forgetting that if I could just stick with the pack, then I could overtake them in the end.

Felicity was in the sixth lane and shot ahead of everyone immediately. I kept my eyes on lane two, pumping my arms and legs in unison while I crept up on her then passed her around the next corner. *One down, six to go.* I was *not* coming in last today.

I locked my eyes on lane three as we flew down the straightaway. On the third corner, I overtook her and switched my focus to lane four. *Two down.* I didn't even bother looking for Felicity. I could see someone pulling farther ahead from the pack out of the corner of my eye and assumed it was her.

My legs burned, but they stayed strong. I leaned into the bend the way a motorcycle leans into a curve in the road and passed lane four. *Three down.* I forced myself to take deeper breaths than I wanted to maintain my speed. Felicity was already halfway down the last straightaway. *Dammit.* I flew around the corner and into the last hundred meters of the track. My strength was waning as I desperately tried to catch lane five, but I could also feel the other runners breathing down my neck. I crossed the finish line in fifth place.

Fifth place isn't last place, I tried to reassure myself. Every step I took shook my thighs so badly I thought I might fall over. It felt good to run like that even though the 400-meter was my least favorite race. When I was running, I wasn't thinking about Lucas, or Jason, or anything at all. *Too bad I can't just run forever.*

The sounds of heavy breathing were all around me as the other seven runners caught their breath while we cooled off with a walk around the track. My legs had stopped shaking, but the lactic acid buildup was causing cramping. I stepped off the track and onto the grass to stretch my legs before I couldn't walk anymore. Felicity came over and plopped down on the grass beside me.

"Hey, Olivia! You were looking good out there." She nodded at the track.

"I'm working on it. Nowhere near as fast as you are, though."

She shrugged. Too polite to agree, but too talented to argue.

"Coach Addison really seems to be working us harder lately." Now she nodded to where he was standing, clipboard in hand as usual.

"Yeah, well, he promised me he was going to have fun making my life miserable." I smirked and finished stretching out my calves, then stood up to bounce on the balls of my feet to make sure the pain had receded. "Ready?" I reached out to help her up and her gaze turned suspicious. I knew I deserved that. I hadn't exactly been overly friendly to her.

She grabbed my hand and let me pull her up. "Ready."

We walked the last half of the track together in silence and joined the rest of the team, who were all stretching on the track. Coach Addison looked almost… excited. His eyes sparkled more than usual, and he had a fresh spring in his step. I wasn't sure whether I should be happy or terrified.

"Okay, team, I have a big announcement," he started. "A special track meet for the entire county is happening in seven weeks, just after Christmas break, the purpose of which is to scout up-and-coming talent. They're looking for the best of the best."

I fought the urge to tune him out. I used to be the best of the best but hadn't been lately. I listened but certainly didn't share his enthusiasm.

"I've been tracking the times of different runners across the county and, honestly, our team is at the top for speed and stamina. We are the favorites to win." He smiled at Felicity and a few other stars of the team. I couldn't help but notice his eyes gloss right over me. I ran my hand along the track absentmindedly. "This next part particularly interests the handful of high school seniors we have on the team." My head shot up. "The overall winners of the girls and boys seventeen to eighteen age groups will win a spot in the AMN elite running program, which guarantees each runner a full scholarship to one of three colleges."

He held up three fingers for dramatic effect.

I shot my hand straight in the air. He gave me a withering look and pointed at me so I could ask my question.

"What schools?" I held my breath.

He checked his clipboard. "The University of Ft. Lauderdale, The University of Tampa, and Carleton University in New York."

The coach continued speaking, but my mind was racing. I knew this could pay for my schooling so that my parents wouldn't have to worry about it. But could I do it? I waited until after practice to talk to him. I knew he'd be straight with me. If I had no chance, then I'd deal with that, but if there was even the slightest hope…

I stood in front of him twenty minutes later, essentially blocking his path. The rest of the team had already left, and his gym bag was over his shoulder. "Coach Addison, could I have a word?"

"What is it, Olivia?" He stood tapping his foot impatiently, waiting for me to speak.

"Do you think I have a shot of winning a spot in AMN?" I didn't beat around the bush—he wasn't a man who appreciated someone not getting to the point as fast as possible—and bit my lip as I waited for his answer.

His eyebrows creased together, and I could see that he was really considering it.

"The Olivia of today? No." He watched me as I nodded my disappointment slowly.

"Okay, coach. Thanks anyway." I shrugged as though I weren't fighting the urge to burst into tears.

"See, that's the problem, Olivia. *Can* you do it? Sure. *Will* you do it? I don't know."

I stopped and looked at him again. "I'm not sure what you mean."

"The Olivia that Coach Stewart promised me when you joined this team—*she* could win—but you? You're distracted and unmotivated and have been for months." He hitched his duffel bag higher on his shoulder and prepared to leave.

"I know I have been, but not anymore. I'm here for this, coach." My eyes pleaded with him to believe me—and to my surprise, his face softened.

"Look, if you're serious, this is going to take more effort than you've probably ever put into anything in your life. You'll have to work your ass off, and even then it still might not be enough. It's going to feel like boot camp multiplied by a million. You have to fight like hell for anything worth having. Don't come to practice thinking I owe you anything. My focus is on helping the athletes I feel have the best chance to win and right now, that's not you. If you don't work, you don't win; it's just that simple. This isn't some childhood fairytale where you can show up on race day and magically transform into the best runner on the team. That's how little kids think, and you are not a little kid."

He nodded at me after this speech, clapped my shoulder and left.

I began a slow walk around the track as tears welled up in my eyes. I was disappointed in his answer though impressed by his diplomacy. *That's how little kids think, and you are not a little kid.* I wanted to kick something. I hadn't found what I was looking for with Jason or Ali. I couldn't stay with Lucas, I'd been useless at *h*elping Mela and had only burdened my parents more all the time.

Deciding to start a light jog around the track, I told myself I had to succeed *at somethin*g. Perhaps Coach Addison didn't think I had a chance to win right now but I knew someone who would. If I could convince him to help me train then maybe, just maybe, I would have a shot at winning and getting that scholarship. There was only one way to find out.

21

I stood outside of a cozy little cottage-like bungalow. The well-kept house before me, the beds blooming with flowers and the clean pond told me that the man I had come to see was finding peace in his retirement, and I might have a hard time getting him out of it.

The door opened and an older gentleman in a red and white matching track suit, striking blue eyes, and a shock of white hair stood before me.

"Olivia?" He stumbled back a step.

"Coach Stewart. It's nice to see you again." I smiled warmly at my old coach.

"*What* are you doing here?" He clutched his chest dramatically, as though I had just given him the surprise of his life.

"I need your help. May I come in?"

"Of course." He moved aside to let me in.

His home opened directly into his living room, and it felt like I had just walked onto the set of a Pinterest ad. Cream-colored blankets and throw pillows rested delicately on the matching leather furniture. A large sign with black script over a white background read *Our Adventure* and a dozen pictures hung in matching frames; I guessed they were of his family, including grandchildren. The walls of the living room were a gentle shade of almond and a beautiful stone fireplace held large flameless candles for ambiance. I glanced into the kitchen and saw that it was spotless, with a single coffee mug drying on a rack. Everything felt so meticulous.

"Your home is beautiful." I couldn't hide my surprise.

"Yes, my Mabel took care of the decor, and I've just kept it up since she passed. She trained me well." His eyes crinkled playfully as he gazed at their wedding picture on the wall.

"Oh, I'm so sorry for your loss. I didn't realize..." I felt terrible for dropping in unannounced.

"Don't do that," he murmured.

"Do what?" I questioned.

"Pity me. She was sick for a long time before she died six months ago, and we had over fifty years together. I miss her every day, but I'm still going. My rose bushes won't tend to themselves." His bottom lip quivered slightly, and I pretended not to notice. "So, what can I do for you?"

I nodded quickly. "I need you to train me."

"Train you? I already did that, my dear." He tilted his head at me.

"I know you did, but I'm out of shape. The track meet to get into the AMN elite running program is in seven weeks and I need to win, but I can't do that right now." I took the seat on the couch as he sat heavily on the recliner to my left.

"Out of shape? Since when?" He was looking at me as though I had two heads.

"It's been a tough year. I mean... who am I talking to? Of course, it doesn't compare to losing your wife." I backtracked immediately. *Really smooth, Liv.*

"Olivia, I already gave you all my training tips and routines last year so that you could get onto the Lion's track team. Just go back through that training schedule and you'll be in tiptop shape in no time. Drink?" He stood and headed to the kitchen.

He was moving more slowly and deliberately than I had ever

seen him. For the first time in the years I'd known him, he looked… old. I accepted the glass of water he offered me, took a sip, and set it down on the coffee table in front of us. I needed him to train me, but how could I convince him?

"So how is the Lion's team?" He scooted back in his chair and rested his ankle on his knee.

"Umm… it's okay, I guess. Not like at Gibbons. Coach Addison is a very different coach than you are."

"Was. I retired last year." His tone was of equal parts relief and longing.

"Retired? Well, you're still a coach. I just think that I could really excel under your guidance again."

He gave me a knowing look. "Why can't coach Addison guide you to victory?"

"He's great, but he has other athletes to focus on and I need more one-on-one coaching." I chose my words carefully. I didn't want to admit that Addison didn't think I had a shot of winning at the moment, but I suspected Coach Stewart knew even without my confession.

"Coach Addison doesn't like you until he respects you. What makes you think you'd do any better working with me if you've had such an off year?" As he folded his arms, I knew I was losing him.

I leaned forward. "I just know it would be different. You've always understood me, and I *have* to win."

"Why do you *have* to win?"

"I don't think my parents can afford college for me, and if I win I'm guaranteed a scholarship." It wasn't the whole truth, but I hoped it was enough.

"Running is hard work, Olivia, and if you're that out of shape, I don't know what you'd expect in a mere seven weeks. I'm not even sure I have it in me. Sorry, but it's a no."

He stood up and invited me to see the new greenhouse he had built in the backyard. I followed, a little dejected.

The greenhouse was an extensive structure made of plastic

sheeting on a wooden frame. We walked through the door, and it was instantly much warmer than outside. He had lined trays of seedlings on wire racks, each labelled in neat script. Herbs, spices, flowers, fruit, and vegetables were all growing. The shoots were green and seemed to be thriving. He had hung beautiful plants on hooks in each corner. The sun streamed through the clear roof and lit up condensation beads on the plastic walls. Birds chirped outside and the wind blew through the trees. It was very peaceful.

"You've done a really amazing job here, Coach Stewart. You've got a gift of helping things grow." I smiled at my obvious double meaning. I wasn't taking no for an answer.

"My Mabel always wanted her own greenhouse. It was something we were going to enjoy working on together once we had the time. I suppose perhaps we shouldn't have waited so long. Now I've built it in honor of her memory instead of with her, and I would have much preferred the latter." His eyes glistened with tears, and I squeezed his arm gently.

We both needed this. Maybe if we worked together, we could distract each other.

"Coach, I lost myself this year. My best friend lost her mom, and I've struggled to know how to support her. I spent a year tracking down my birth father and when I met him it was... disappointing. My boyfriend and I broke up, and I just feel a bit lost." I cleared my throat to mask the slew of emotions that were rising in me. "Running has always been my haven. It's the thing I do best. Right now, it feels like it's all I have left. I know that if I focus and train really hard, then I might have a real shot at winning, but I need a coach who believes in me. I need a coach who is on my side and knows that I can do this as much as I do. Haven't you ever felt like if you could just fix that one thing, then everything else would fall into place?" I held my breath as he stared at me. This was it. If he said no now, I'd have to give up.

We stood in his greenhouse facing each other for what felt

like a really long time. Things he had patiently nurtured and cared for surrounded us. Plants he had willed to grow and gently cheered on until they thrived on their own. It's what he had done for me, and the irony was not lost.

"Morewood track, from five to seven a.m. every single day of the week for the next seven weeks. You will not miss a day, you will not complain, and we will get you that scholarship together." His eyes twinkled as I threw my arms around him in a display of affection that caught us both by surprise.

I quickly pulled away. "Sorry, and thank you so much. You won't regret this." I couldn't wipe the grin off my face.

"I know that, Olivia. It's what Mabel would have wanted. And besides, if I don't start getting out of the house more, I'm going to become the crazy plant man everyone avoids."

His booming laughter filled the greenhouse and reminded me of the man I'd known before he lost his wife.

"I'll see you tomorrow then?" I wanted to go tell Mela the good news as soon as I could. We both needed a win.

"Five a.m. Don't be late." He picked up his watering can and began putzing around the plants again.

I practically sprinted to my car and drove directly to Mela's.

Fifteen minutes later, we were sitting on her bed with our usual brands of ice cream, only this time we were celebrating instead of crying together the way we had been for weeks on end.

"So he's going to train you one on one?" Mela's mouth was full of caramel swirl ice cream, and she was in jeans and a tank top, which was an enormous improvement from the constant cycle of sweatpants and stained t-shirts she'd been wearing lately.

I spoke through my mouthful of raspberry ripple. "Yeah, starting tomorrow."

"That's great, Liv. You think you'll beat Felicity?"

"Probably not, but I don't have to. She's only sixteen, so she's not in my age category." *Thank God for that.*

Mela nodded. "Have you told Lucas?" Her eyes grew wide, the way they did when she asked about something she knew was off limits but doing it anyway.

"Mel..."

She had not agreed with my decision to break up with Lucas, but at least it had proven to be a great distraction for her, as we argued back and forth about it.

"How long are you going to let this go on for?"

"We're done, Mel. We're just not on the same page anymore." I took another bite, but the ice cream tasted flavorless in my mouth. "How are *you* doing?" I changed the subject and searched her face for signs of dishonesty. I knew her dad was still working as much as possible, and several times a week she stayed over at my place.

"It's getting better. I didn't cry until noon today, and it only lasted a few minutes. Plus, you know, I showered and look fantastic today."

We looked at each other and grinned.

"You do look amazing. Hot date?" I smirked.

"Yeah, actually. You know, we could make it a double, just say the word." She hopped off the bed and grabbed our ice cream containers.

I recognized the faint fire behind her eyes and was glad for it, however misplaced it was. Wrapping my arms around her, I pinned hers down as she held the ice cream.

"Have fun tonight," I whispered.

I pulled away and laughed at the look on her face.

"Uh, thanks, weirdo." She shook her head with a smile on her face.

The days had been longer and sadder lately, so I really noticed when a good one happened. Today had definitely been a good day.

22

"Yes, Olivia!"

Coach Stewart clicked the stopwatch to record my time for the last run of our session as I flew across the finish line. His matching track suit was light blue today and complemented his eyes, but it was just a blur of color as I sped by.

I slowed my run to a walk and turned around to head back to where he stood. I was struggling to get control of my breathing.

"Better?" I asked.

"See for yourself."

He turned the stopwatch toward me and I whistled. In the last three weeks of daily training, I had shaved off over four seconds of my time for the 400-meter race. I looked up, and his expression confused me.

"Why are you looking at me like that?" I sucked in breaths between each word.

"Olivia, this seems to be about more than just a scholarship."

My cheeks flushed. "I don't know what you mean."

"What are you thinking about when you're running?" he asked gently.

"I don't know. I mean, I'm thinking about how much I love

running. How great it feels, and how I'd like to just run forever." I stood up, having caught my breath.

He stroked his chin. "'When I was a child, I talked like a child, I thought like a child, I reasoned like a child. When I became a man, I put the ways of childhood behind me.'"

I stared blankly. "Huh?"

"It's a Bible verse. 1 Corinthians 13:11."

"Okay, but why are you bringing it up?" I hoped he wasn't about to get all religious on me.

"Because, Olivia, if you had put childish things away, then you wouldn't be thinking of running from anything. Instead, you'd be thinking of running *toward* something."

"I never said I was running away."

I stared hard at him, and he gave me a knowing look.

"You didn't have to. What happened when you found your birth father? Why was it disappointing?" He had his working-out-a-hunch face on.

After a moment, I said, "It was disappointing because I was expecting to feel differently. I thought I would meet my birth parents and magically feel complete, and that's not what happened."

"You feel lost." It wasn't a question.

I looked into his kind blue eyes and my defenses melted. "Yes," I whispered.

"May I share my opinion?" His face was sympathetic, so I nodded for him to go on. "It seems to me that you've been carrying around the label of being adopted as though it were a war wound. It cripples you somehow, and I won't pretend to know why; I just know that it does." His voice was warm in a way my dad's often got when he was trying to soothe me.

"I guess I've wanted people to coddle me. To tell me that everything is going to be okay. And the people who really love me have all been there for me. But I haven't really been there for them, and they have problems of their own." My eyes fell to the ground, weighed down by my confession.

He began walking, and I walked with him. "Maybe you need to get some distance from the people you keep relying on to save you. You say you feel lost, so perhaps it's time to go away and find yourself."

"What do you mean?" Where was I supposed to go?

"Isn't New York one of the scholarship options if you win? If you do this the right way, with an open heart and mind, you'd be running toward something incredible instead of trying to escape what's behind you. And Carleton University in New York is known for making people grow—or for chewing them up and spitting them out." He shrugged. "If I was a betting man, and I'm not because Mabel would roll over in her grave, then my money would be on you rising to the challenge instead of shrinking away from it."

Without any other words, he dropped the stopwatch he'd been holding into his gym bag.

"Four laps of cool down, stretch, and then you're done for today." He picked up his bag and began to walk away.

"You're just gonna drop a bomb like 'move to New York' and leave?" My hands were up as if I expected to fill them with something. Detailed instructions on how to get a life?

"I have an appointment." He waggled his eyebrows mysteriously.

"At six forty in the morning?"

"Go. Think about what I said." He pointed to the track, and I raised my arms in surrender as I started my jog.

The sun peeked over the horizon as I began my second lap around the track. The dew on the grass sparkled as the sun's rays hit the blades. *I keep expecting someone to complete me, but everyone is full of their own pain.* Maybe it was up to me. Wasn't that what growing up was all about? "In this world you'll have trouble"—that's what we're promised. Why did I keep expecting fairy tales in a world that promised trouble?

There were butterflies in my stomach. New York? Could I really leave like that? I felt a smile slowly spread across my cheeks. It was far enough away to cut the ties, that was for sure. It would ensure I couldn't keep burdening the same people with my struggles and expecting them to solve everything. If I left, then I could build myself up and come back better. I could figure out exactly who I needed to be so that I could be good to everyone who needed me. To everyone who had been so good to me.

I finished my run and took a long drink of water as I looked back at the track. It wouldn't be easy. I only had four more weeks to get into the best shape of my life.

I could do it. It was time for me to start designing my life instead of living reactively. Time to grow up. The first step was winning that track meet.

"Nice work out there, Olivia. This is the third practice in a row you've come second after Felicity."

Coach Addison was in shorts and a black windbreaker, and if he hadn't said my name, I would have assumed he was talking to someone else. I still pointed to myself in a question.

"Yeah you." He laughed. *He laughed.*

"Wow, thanks coach." It was the third time I had come in behind Felicity and I clenched my fists tightly to keep from punching something. There was only one week until the track meet, and I still couldn't catch her, no matter which race we ran.

"Your time is pacing with the best runners in your age group. What else have you been doing?" Coach Addison was standing in front of me, clipboard at the ready as always, a quizzical look on his face.

"What do you mean?" I was still replaying the race in my

mind trying to pinpoint where I'd messed up, but I couldn't find anything. She was just faster.

"Look, I know I'm a great coach, but there's no way you've improved this much without some kind of additional effort— so out with it." A playful smile tugged at the corners of his mouth. I wasn't used to this version of him, and it was slightly unnerving.

"Oh, I've been training with Coach Stewart every morning for two hours before school." My stomach clenched. I wasn't sure if he'd be ticked off that I had sought outside help.

He stared at me for a few seconds and then waved his arms in the air for the rest of the team to gather around.

"I'm sure you've all noticed the improvement in Olivia's running over the last few weeks, yes?"

Oh crap. Where was he going with this? The team murmured their acknowledgment and my face flushed with embarrassment. Had I been so bad that everyone on the team noticed? He went on.

"She knew she needed more help, so she got it. She's been training an extra fourteen hours each week, and look at the difference. This is what happens when you train with the Lions. You get inspired to work harder and do more." He nodded at me with approval.

I had to fight back a laugh. He had made my improvement all about himself. It was just ridiculous enough to merit a massive belly laugh, but this was the nicest he'd ever been to me, so I held it in. He took my smirk for acknowledgment, and we continued with practice. By the end of it, I was feeling incredible. Coach Addison had said that I was pacing with the best runners in my age group. That was huge. I still hadn't beaten Felicity, but I was getting closer, and I kept reminding myself that I didn't have to beat her to win the scholarship. Still, though, it would feel amazing to do it.

In my car after practice, my phone dinged with a Facebook notification and I nearly didn't check it before driving home but something told me to. When I opened my phone, I nearly let it drop to the floor. There, in my notifications, was a brand-new friend request from my half-sister Leah Riker. I stared at her profile picture in disbelief. That meant Mark must have told her who I was, and that she actually wanted to know me. Warmth spread through my chest and my cheeks began to hurt from the sheer force of my smile. I tapped on it and hit accept. I was now Facebook friends with my biological sister.

23

"What's she like?" Mela was sitting across from me in a booth at Brew during my lunch break.

"She's... amazing."

It was December 27, and we were off for Christmas break. The track meet was next week, and though it was my birthday I had picked up an extra shift. Mela had joined me. Birthdays had always been kind of complicated for me, and this year was worse than usual. After I had accepted Leah's friend request, she'd sent me a message, and we'd been messaging back and forth ever since. My hunch had been right about Mark. He had told her everything he knew and even helped her look me up on Facebook.

"Wow," Mela said for the third time in twenty minutes.

"I know." I was still in shock. Knowing her slightly from a distance and developing a relationship with my biological sister were two very different things. It was like a dream.

She was fourteen, loved music, editing videos with her friends, sunsets over the ocean, and road trips. Most of all, she was kind, like her father was, and unashamed of me. She immediately listed me as a family member on her profile. I would love to have been a fly on the wall when Ali saw that. She looked a lot like me, only with much lighter skin, and she had a dry wit that often made me laugh out loud. She was quickly becoming one of my favorite people.

"This is amazing, Liv. Seriously. Just, like... don't forget about me, okay?" Mela said it with a laugh, but I heard the meaning behind her words.

My eyes bore into hers. "You're my family too, Mel. Sisters, no matter what."

"No matter what," she whispered back.

We'd been saying it for years, but the words had never held as much meaning as they did in that moment. I cleared my throat and glanced at my watch. There was another ten minutes before my break was over. I pulled out my phone and checked my email quickly. There was one from coach Addison that stopped me in my tracks with the subject line: "LAST MINUTE CHANGE TO THE AMN QUALIFICATION TRACK MEET." I opened it immediately.

Team,

There has been a last-minute change to qualify for AMN during next week's track meet. There weren't as many students in the seventeen/eighteen age category as they had originally planned for, so they've opened it up to include the sixteen-year-olds as well. The male and female students between sixteen and eighteen years old with the highest marks overall at the meet will win the spots in AMN and the scholarship that goes with it. Obviously, if a sixteen-year-old wins, they'll defer the scholarship for a year.

Hope you had a nice Christmas. See you at practice.

Coach Addison

• • •

"WHAT'S WRONG? You're as white as a ghost." Mela was leaning across the table, about to slap my face.

I had never beaten Felicity before, and now it was the only way to win. Losing was not an option, but my confidence from the last couple of weeks dissolved in an instant.

"They changed the rules to qualify for AMN." My voice was barely audible.

"Changed how?" Mela's eyes narrowed.

"Felicity can qualify now. It's over." I bit my lip to keep it from trembling. I would not fall apart about this in the middle of a shift.

"What? Can they do that?" She was appropriately furious on my behalf.

"Yeah. It's their game. They can do what they want." I sank lower into my seat and tossed my phone into my purse with disgust.

"Okay, I can see you circling the drain here. You've been coming in behind her, right?"

I nodded glumly.

"Liv, that's a tremendous improvement from fifth a few weeks ago. Don't spiral on me. You can still do this."

I looked away so that Mela wouldn't see the guilt on my face. "Mel—" I still hadn't told her that my plan was to leave. There was really no perfect time to tell your best friend you wanted to move across the country to be alone.

"You are going to kick her butt, and Nate and I will be there to celebrate with you." She stood up and squeezed my shoulder as she left me to finish my shift.

I went through the last two hours like a zombie. All my plans were contingent on me winning that scholarship. I didn't have a Plan B because Plan A *had* to work. This was the only way that I could become who I needed to be and have my parents off the hook for my tuition fees. It was foolproof, as long as I won. Felicity could ruin everything if I didn't deliver.

I whipped the cloth I was holding into the sink, ran the water to clean the sides and watched it slowly swirl down the drain. *Just like your plans.*

I checked my watch, and to my surprise my shift had ended thirty minutes ago. The optional track practice was starting in ten minutes, and I didn't have any intention of missing it. I quickly changed into my running gear and headed over to the track. I arrived a few minutes late and snuck unnoticed onto the track to stretch with everyone. Felicity, who hadn't noticed me because she was chatting with another girl, was a few feet in front of me.

"… so excited to win next week. As soon as I read the email, I knew it was a done deal." She leaned forward to touch her toes.

"What about Olivia? She's been catching up to you, hasn't she?"

I could have kissed Taylor for saying it. She was a relatively recent addition to the team, and though we'd never really talked, we'd always exchanged pleasantries with each other.

"Olivia *Jackson*?" Felicity said my last name like she had to think about who I was. "I wrote her off the first week she got here. She's got some talent for sure, but she's not motivated. Not like I am. She let herself get distracted over a *boy* all summer and she's had to play catch up. Maybe if she had a few more months to train, she could give me a run for my money, but she said it herself—she's nowhere near as fast as I am." She raised her arm over her head and pulled her elbow with her other arm to stretch.

Taylor's red ponytail bobbed from side to side as she shook her head. She turned her head slightly so she could see me and rolled her eyes. All this time, I thought Felicity had been this sweet younger girl who couldn't help it if she was the best in our running age group. I hadn't realized she simply never saw me as a threat. The team was comprised of different age groups because it was an elite running club open to anyone from ages fourteen to twenty-two, so the coach divided us by age. I had been running against Felicity since the beginning, and I had never wanted to beat her more than right this second.

We stood up to get started and as she turned and made eye contact with me, her face registered awareness that I had heard what she said. She smiled innocently and gave a little shrug, as though she had been playing around. I knew better. Coach Addison blew his whistle, and the team began the warm-up jog. I walked past Taylor, who had let Felicity run ahead.

"I'd pay good money to watch you kick her butt at the meet," Taylor muttered into my ear.

"That's the plan." I stared straight ahead.

They would not write me off. Not Felicity, not Coach Addison, not my old principal, not Ali or Chris, or even Jason. I was the underdog, and not seeing me as a threat was a mistake.

24

"Welcome, everyone, to the Broward County track meet. Each competitor will compete in three races and two field events. There will be three heats and a last race for each running event. We will select the winners based on points. Three points for a first-place finish, two points for a second-place finish, and one point for a third-place finish. We will tally the points at the end of the event and announce the winners. We will award ribbons for first, second, and third place in each age group. For the sixteen- to eighteen-year-old competitors, representatives from the AMN elite running program are here and will award the winners of the male and female age group with a spot in their spring program. Good luck, everyone!"

The loudspeaker switched off, and I stood near Coach Addison, shifting my weight from one foot to the other.

I was in spandex shorts and my black and gold Lion's jersey. My hair was in a tight ponytail, and I had been up since four a.m., stretching and warming up. I was as ready as I'd ever be. I could see Mela and Nate in the bleachers with two gigantic neon signs. Mela's read "Go, Olivia, Go!" and Nate's read, "Olivia Jackson for president!" I wasn't sure Nate really got the whole track scene, but his sign had brought a smile to my face, for which I was grateful.

"Okay, team, here are your event schedules." Coach Addison handed each of us a sheet of paper with a schedule of all the events, along with their times and our names beside the events we'd be competing in.

I scanned it quickly for my name and found my events. 100-meter dash, 200-meter, 400-meter, long jump, and triple jump. The qualifying heats for the races were in the morning and the finals in the afternoon. My first race was the 100-meter dash in thirty minutes. I felt a surge of gratitude toward Coach Stewart for insisting I practice long and triple jump every day. I looked around but didn't see him anywhere, which surprised me. He had said he'd be at the meet for the whole day.

"Olivia, come here for a second." Coach Addison was waving me over.

"Yeah, Coach?" I bounced on the balls of my feet.

"Do you feel good about your events?"

"Everything but the 400-meter. I just haven't mastered that one yet." I figured honesty was better than fake confidence.

He nodded in agreement. "Yeah, I was going to choose a different race, but Coach Stewart insisted on the 400."

"Coach Stewart? He chose my events?" *And you let him?*

"He did. We met a couple of weeks ago to discuss it. Just keep your head in the game today." He patted my shoulder affectionately.

"Thanks, Coach." I smiled up at him before walking away to stretch again.

"Oh, and Olivia? I like you just fine." He smirked and headed off to talk to a different team member.

Heat flooded my cheeks, and I made a mental note to discuss the coaching code of conduct with Coach Stewart the next time I saw him. Fifteen minutes later, I lined up on the track, waiting for my heat assignment. The top two in each heat went to the final automatically, so that's what I aimed for. Felicity was first in her heat right before my run, and I put it out of my mind. I couldn't focus on her all day, or I'd trail behind.

"On your mark!"

I readied myself into the starting block in my lane. The very top of my tiptoes were the only thing in the blocks.

"Set!"

I expertly placed my fingers behind the line. My thumb and index held my weight as I stared down the track. The gun went off, and I was out of the blocks like a shot. My arms and legs pumped in unison, the adrenaline coursing through my body as it carried me across the finish line first in my heat. As the race attendant took my jersey number, I slowed down my breathing. Though it was just the first race, and it was only a qualifying heat, I was having to hold back a giant *whoop*. I could hear Mela screaming like I had just won the Olympics. I waved and jogged back to where our team had set up for the day.

"Well done, Olivia." I beamed at Coach Stewart, who had appeared out of thin air. "One down. Now let's focus on triple jump." His track suit was lime green, and he stood out like a sore thumb.

"Why did you insist on the 400? I don't know if I can—" He put his hand up to stop me.

"You're getting ahead of yourself. Let's take this one event at a time. Next is the triple jump. Got it?" His eyes were as severe as I'd ever seen them.

I nodded soberly. He had gotten me this far, and I had to trust that he knew best.

"That's better. Okay, there are no do-overs in the field events. Whatever you place is what you place, so you've got to make sure you give it your all. You only get two jumps, no practice or retakes. Got it?"

"Got it." I knew the drill. It never made things easier, but it was nice having a personal escort to each of my events.

I had done this event so many times in the last seven weeks that I had been jumping in my sleep. I walked over to the board that I would spring from, turned around and counted my steps back to the spot I would start at and put a piece of duct tape down on the runway. A couple of girls snickered, but I tuned them out. I had practiced this again and again, down to the exact step I needed to start on.

Out of fourteen jumpers, I was the ninth. I sat on the grass stretching while I waited for my turn to jump. I tuned everything else out and did not know what the rest of the field was jumping. It was between me and the sandpit, and that was it. On my turn, I placed my right foot down on the duct tape and put my left leg behind it. Everyone else faded as I stared at the sandpit at the end of the track. I bent my legs and used my arms to pump me forward with momentum as I ran down the stretch of track toward the first board. My right foot landed on it perfectly. I swung my arms and drove my left leg into the air and landed on my left foot, then swung my arms again and bounded off with my right foot straight into the sand.

It was a good jump. I could tell by the look on the faces of the scorekeepers. Was it enough for first, though? I couldn't be sure until all the girls jumped.

"Okay, ladies. You have one more jump. The current standings are as follow: In first place, we have Krista Walker with a jump of thirty-eight feet, two inches. In second place, we have Olivia Jackson with a jump of thirty-seven feet flat. In third place, we have Laura Veener with a jump of thirty-two feet, five inches. We'll go in the same order as before, so please line up." The blond lady with the clipboard looked official.

Coach Stewart waved me over.

"You can do better than that. Just break forty feet, and you've got this." He looked much more confident than I felt.

"Right. Just jump farther than I ever have before. Got it." I grimaced, and he smacked my shoulder encouragingly, as if to say, *that's the spirit.*

The first-place jumper was just ahead of me. She must have been at least five foot eight and had the longest legs I'd ever seen, which seemed like an unfair advantage, considering I was barely over five feet tall. I knew I would have to rely on my speed and strength. Sure, I didn't have long lanky legs, but I had legs as strong as tree trunks. I could do this.

She finished her jump and was smiling. *Damn. It's fine. I'm a Lion. We're the team to beat.* I stepped onto the runway and immediately thought of the battle scene from every movie where the hero thrusts his sword into the air and screams, "For Narnia!" Or whatever they're fighting for. I raised my hands in the air and internally screamed, "For college!" And though I knew it was stupid, like really stupid, it made me feel stronger somehow—and I flew into my jump even faster than the first time.

Waiting for the results was the hardest part, so I decided not to. I knew I had given it my all. I couldn't have jumped any farther if I tried, so I signaled to Coach Stewart and we left. The results would be there later, and I couldn't stress about what points I had or didn't have. All I could do was leave it all on the track, and so that's what I did.

By the end of the day, I had qualified for all three running finals and finished my long-jump event. Nate and Mela were troopers, having skipped the entire day of school to cheer me on. After they found the canteen, I saw them with fries, shakes, and chips. I knew if I looked closely enough, I'd see some candy in the midst as well. I smiled to myself, grateful that they had come.

The 100-meter final was starting, and I was in lane four, directly beside Felicity. Coach Stewart had warned me they had mixed the ages for the finals, but it was still a shock to see her standing there and stretching.

"Olivia, well done. You made it to the final." That she sounded so surprised made me want to hit something.

Instead, I smiled sweetly and said, "I made it to all the finals, actually."

Her eyes popped a little, but she immediately recovered, no doubt reassuring herself that I still wasn't any competition to her. "Well, good luck."

"You too." I turned to face the straightaway.

I'd have to tune her out if I had any chance of winning. We lined up in the starting blocks and I took off as soon as the gun sounded, but it wasn't enough. I stayed with Felicity right up to the last ten meters, and then she slowly pulled ahead just enough to win.

"Marcelli in first, followed by Jackson in second, and Hayes in third."

I didn't know who made the announcement, and it didn't matter. Second. It might as well have been last. The 200-meter final went exactly the same way. Felicity in first, me in second. It was over. No college, no escape. I walked off the track with my shoulders slumped and sat by myself on the long-jump runway since no one was using it anymore. It had been a long day, and though it wasn't officially over, it felt that way. A shadow fell over me as someone stood directly above.

"Olivia, what are you doing over here? You should prep for the 400 final." Coach Stewart sounded annoyed.

"Yeah, sorry. Just needed a minute." My voice was quiet, and my shoulders still slumped. I felt terrible for letting him down.

"Listen, all you need to do is stay with Felicity through to the 300 mark, and then make your move. She's steady, but she wanes at the end." His voice was low, like he was telling me top-secret information.

"So do I, Coach. Besides, it doesn't really matter anymore, right?" My shoulders were sinking deeper and deeper as we walked. Any farther down, and I'd be crawling.

"Do you not know?" Coach Stewart had stopped and pulled my arm to stop me too.

"Know what?" Did *he* not know that I had blown two races?

"Olivia, how many times do I need to remind you to keep track of everyone's scores at a track meet? Including your competition." He sighed and aggressively pulled a folded sheet of paper out of his back pocket. "You and Felicity are currently tied for first overall." He pointed to the sheet where he had circled Felicity's name and mine in red and written the number ten beside each.

"Tied? How?" I could feel the hope beginning to grow, but I was trying to stuff it down. He must have miscalculated.

"Felicity placed second in both of her field events." He said it matter-of-factly, as though that should answer my confusion.

"Okay…" I narrowed my eyes, trying to understand.

"Have you not even been keeping track of your *own* scores?"

My cheeks flushed with embarrassment. It had seemed like the right decision, but now it felt incredibly stupid.

"You placed first, Olivia. In both long jump *and* triple jump. Whichever one of you places higher in the 400 will win the spot in AMN." His expression made me wonder if I had just grown a second head. He still couldn't believe I didn't know.

I felt a nervous excitement growing within me. I could still win this. *All you need to do is stay with Felicity through to the 300 mark and then make your move.* Stay with her? Easier said than done, but I would do my best. We walked back to where the rest of the team was sitting together.

"Jackson, you should be really proud of your efforts today. You've done well." Coach Addison sounded as if he were congratulating me after the day was done.

"Well, I still have the 400-meter final to run."

"Right. Yeah, I'm just saying. No matter how things go, you should be really proud." He patted my head and walked away.

I stood still and silent as fury swept through me. He didn't think I could win. He assumed Felicity would win. Even after his encouragement this morning, he was still Team Felicity.

Well, he can shove his well wishes. I caught Coach Stewart's eye on my way back to the track, and he nodded with understanding.

"Use that rage, Olivia."

I gave him a single nod back. *I intend to.*

25

"*On your mark!*"

The eight runners on the track stepped in front of their starting blocks, me included. I was in lane one and Felicity in lane eight. The rest of the track didn't matter to me. It was me versus lane eight. I settled into my blocks the same way I did for every race. Toes at the bottom, spikes pushing against the rubber pedals, arms shoulder-width apart, fingertips touching the rubber track just behind the starting line.

"*Set!*"

Thighs up in the air waiting for the gun. *Pace yourself Jackson.* I could hear Coach Stewart's words in my head. I couldn't afford to burn out too quickly. The gun went off, and every runner on the track was in motion. My spikes gripped the rubber track and pulled me forward effortlessly. I leaned into the first corner, and Felicity was way ahead. *She started in lane eight. Of course she's ahead.*

I thought of Coach Addison's words that day after practice. *You have to fight like hell for anything worth having.* And suddenly it hit me. This race wasn't about Felicity. This was my chance to spread my wings. I flew down the straightaway and stopped looking at anyone else. They didn't matter. I used to compete with only myself because that was all that had mattered. This race wasn't about me versus her, it was about me versus me.

I rounded the third corner and felt my legs ask for relief. Me versus me. The old me who needed others to coddle her and be able to depend on them, versus the me I wanted to be. The me who would be independent. Who would stop relying on the same people over and over again. The me who would leave so she could come back and break the perpetual cycles that needed breaking.

Felicity and I rounded the last corner, but because I was in the first lane and she in the eighth, I had less track to cover as I raced into the straightaway ahead of her. I heard a gasp of disbelief as the balls of my feet pounded against the track and the finish line came into view. I could see her gaining in my peripheral. Only fifty meters to go, and we were neck and neck.

You fight for others so damn hard. Lucas's eyes had been blazing when he had said it. He was right, and I knew I was still fighting for others even now. The starfish necklace he had given me bounced against my chest as I pumped my arms and legs past their breaking point and leaned into the finish line with everything I had.

Coach Stewart was there to catch me right before I collapsed. He eased me down gently onto the track.

"That was one hell of a run, kid." His voice was thick with emotion, and I looked up to find that his eyes were wet with tears.

"Did I do it?" I whispered.

"Let's find out." He pulled me to my feet and let me lean on him as we walked over to the inside of the track, where they had already set up the tri-level podium.

The races were finished for both the guys and the girls, and the officials with their clipboards convened to sort out the winners. Each track team stood together, facing the podium, as a man in a suit came forward and tapped the microphone he was holding.

I glanced over to wave at Mela in the bleachers, and my hand froze in the air as my eyes connected with Lucas's, who was sitting on the other side of Nate. He smiled at me, and a thousand thoughts ran through my mind. I simply let my hand fall and smiled back at him.

"First, I want to congratulate all the athletes who competed in today's events. You were all tremendous."

The man in the suit allowed for clapping.

"We are going to award all the events, and then we will announce the overall male and female winners in the sixteen- to eighteen-age categories."

He began calling each winner's name for first, second, and third place in the field events. I stood at the top of the podium and collected my ribbons for long jump and triple jump. Mela, Nate, and Lucas whooped with enthusiasm each time. Finally, he was calling the winners for the races. I collected my second-place ribbons for the 100- and 200-meter races and then waited with bated breath for him to call the winner of the 400-meter race.

"The winner of the 400-meter race is also the overall winner for the female sixteen- to eighteen-age category and has won the female spot in the AMN elite spring running program." He fumbled with his clipboard, and I couldn't watch. I looked back over at Mela and saw her fingers crossed on both hands. And though I knew I would pay for it later, I risked another glance at Lucas. He looked as nervous as I felt. Our eyes met just as they announced the winner. I saw it in his smile before it registered in my brain.

"Olivia Jackson, congratulations!"

My hand flew to my mouth as Mela hopped up and down in the bleachers. I turned to Coach Stewart, who was smiling widely and wiping his eyes, and I flung my arms around him.

"Thank you." I whispered.

"It was all you, Olivia." He whispered back, and nudged me toward the front.

"Never doubted you for a second, Jackson."

I rolled my eyes at Coach Addison as I took my spot at the top of the podium and let them put a medal around my neck. I looked out over the sea of people and felt a surge of pride. It took everything I had, but I succeeded, and now the actual work was about to begin.

Later, I met with the representative from AMN, and he gave me a registration packet and congratulated me on my win. I felt like I was floating. I had actually done it.

"Do you think you know which school you'll attend in the fall?" The AMN rep asked.

"New York," I answered firmly. He smiled and congratulated me again before leaving.

"New York?"

It came from Mela, who was standing directly behind me.

I winced. She wasn't supposed to find out that way. I turned slowly and faced her.

"Mel, I'm so sorry. I was going to tell you." I bit my lip.

"Why do you want to leave?" Her voice was quiet.

"It's just something I need to do. Besides, you're going to stay with your aunt in Italy for six months after graduation, right?" I was trying and failing to soften the blow.

"Yeah, for six months, not four years."

"I'm sorry, Mel." I pulled her into a hug, and she squeezed back.

"But why?" she whispered as we continued to hug.

I pulled away and looked her in the eye, urging her to understand. "I need to find out who I am on my own. Can you understand that?"

She sighed. "No, not really. What happened with Ali, and Jason, and even Lucas… it was no one's fault, Liv. You *had* to go see your birth parents, and you did. But now it's time to get on with your life and stop driving everyone away. Leaving for New York, it just seems like you're running."

"I'm not running. Not forever, anyway. I can't explain it any more than I have. You just have to trust that I know what I'm doing."

"It's not forever?" Her voice trembled.

"Not a chance." I smiled and pulled her back into a hug.

We walked arm in arm back toward the bleachers. I searched, but I couldn't find him.

"Where are Nate and Lucas?" I tried to keep the burning curiosity out of my voice.

"Lucas had to go, so Nate went with him. They said to tell you congrats, though."

My heart sank, though I knew it was for the best. His being there had meant so much to me, but it didn't suddenly erase all the reasons we had broken up. I looked around the track and smiled at the beautiful glow on the starting blocks cast by the setting sun. I listened to the buzz and excitement of people running up to each other, the sounds of laughter, the tears of disappointment.

On the track, I knew exactly who I was. Fierce, determined, motivated. But off the track, my footing was less sure. Everything would be so different in the fall, and that was the point. It was time to discover who I was away from the comfort of home. If I was lucky, maybe I would find a way to be deserving of the friendships and relationships I had been taking for granted.

EPILOGUE

"You're not gonna puke in my cab, are you?"

The driver's dark eyes darted back and forth from me to the road in front of him through the rearview mirror.

I took a deep breath before answering. "No. Sorry, there are just a lot more people here than I expected." I wrung my hands to keep them from shaking.

People were everywhere. Fancy businessmen on cell phones, high-fashion women walking down the sidewalk in impossibly high heels, groups of young adults hanging out together, others standing in line at various food carts. I had never seen so many people just walking around a city before. I breathed in through my nose and out through my mouth to dispel the feeling of claustrophobia threatening to take over.

The Brooklyn Bridge loomed majestically over New York City's East River, linking the two boroughs of Manhattan and Brooklyn. Since we needed to get over to the Manhattan side, we pulled onto the bridge, and I stared out the now open window—the driver seemed to think I needed some air—at the cables spiderwebbing magnificently in front of the arches. It was breathtaking, or maybe I was still hyperventilating from the claustrophobia.

I snapped a picture with my phone and sent it to Mela. I had already sent her pictures of a very blurry Statue of Liberty from the plane, the airport, a sign for Manhattan, and three pictures of the bridge, each getting progressively closer to it. My plane had been delayed, so it was dusk already and the lights from the hundreds of buildings were reflected on the river. It was beautiful but daunting.

My phone buzzed with a text from Mela.

Okay, okay, I get it. Your new life is picture-perfect. I'm going to sleep now, it's late in ITALY!

I sent one back. Bwahahaha! Yeah, yeah. Your new life is pretty perfect too. I miss you like crazy though.

I COULD SEE the dots indicating she was responding.

Same. FaceTime me tomorrow when you're settled in. Ciao Bella.

I LOCKED my phone and sighed. I did miss her. Maybe I should have stayed in Florida. *At least give it more than five seconds, Liv.* Besides, it's not like Mela was actually in Florida right now. She had already been in Italy visiting her aunt for two weeks.

"So, you're going to Carleton?" The driver seemed satisfied enough that I wasn't going to throw up for the moment.

"Yeah. Full scholarship." I added the second part almost as if explaining how I could afford to be in such a city. I continued to peer out the window at the river and breathed in the smell of exhaust from the slow-moving vehicles all around us. It was better than the stench of hot garbage that had assaulted me throughout Brooklyn.

"Impressive. First year?" he inquired.

"Uh-huh."

We were almost into Manhattan. The nerves in my stomach felt like they would soon rip through it like an ulcer. Maybe I was just hungry. I hoped that was it and that I wouldn't have to seek medical attention an hour into arriving.

"First time to New York, huh?" It was more of a statement than a question.

"Yes, sir." I had no idea why I called him sir. But it was out there, so I left it.

"You'll want to check out Pier 15 if you want a stellar view of the bridge. Lots of students like to study there." His voice was kind and his New York accent thick.

My heart leapt at the thought of having a body of water to stare at again. I was already missing the ocean. I threw him a grateful smile.

"Thank you. Sorry, I'm just really nervous. I don't know anyone here." I immediately regretted telling him that.

What if he was some kind of serial killer and now he knew that I was alone in a strange city? What if he disposed of my body and no one ever found me? My parents would be devastated. And Mela, oh my gosh, she's been through so much. She couldn't lose her best friend too.

"Here we are." I jumped at the sound of his voice.

"Oh! Thank you. Thank you so much." I paid the fare and gave him an extra tip as a thank you for leaving me alive.

I hitched my backpack on my shoulders and gratefully took

my two suitcases from the driver after he had pulled them out of the trunk. The building before me was so high my neck nearly cramped. It looked to be a skyscraper and I would have assumed I was in the wrong place, but "Robertson Hall Residence" was written in large, shiny gold letters above the double doors.

Standing on the sidewalk as people hurried by me from both directions, I waited for a break in traffic and then dragged my suitcases to the wall of the building and tried to stay out of people's way. Should I go directly in or get something to eat first? I wasn't sure I was ready to face my new reality yet. The smell of hot dogs had me sniffing the air appreciatively, and less than two feet away was a bright orange cart with a dancing hot dog on its banner. My stomach growled, and I glanced around before lugging my suitcases over to the cart.

"What can I get ya?" The vendor was a skinny bald guy in his mid-thirties with a black apron and white t-shirt.

"A hot dog please."

"Yeah, I gathered as much. Just the one?"

"Yep." I paid, took the hot dog from him, and then added my toppings while keeping a close eye on my luggage. This was New York City after all.

The building, and my unknown future, loomed to my right. I tried not to look at it but the soft glow of the lights from the windows called to me like a moth to a flame, and I wondered if I would meet the same demise. The outside of the bottom of the building was made up of glass paneling, and I could see people walking around so clearly it might as well have been midday. The rest of the building was light beige, and on the front, there were a hundred and fifty-two windows. Nineteen high and eight across. On the side closest to me, there were only five windows across for a total of ninety-five windows. Assuming my math was correct—and there weren't more hidden windows I couldn't see, that meant there were three-hundred-and-forty-two windows in all. Many of them had lights on which lit the building up like a postcard. It was stunning and made me want to get closer.

I wiped my mouth and tossed my wrapper in the trash. It was easily the best hot dog I'd ever had, but I hardly noticed. I was too busy counting the windows and wondering which one was mine. I had spent so much time daydreaming about what the room would look like that I practically had it memorized. My cheeks hurt and I slowly raised my hand to my face and felt the smile I hadn't realized was there. Now aware of it, I couldn't stop and suddenly I couldn't wait to go into the dorm.

Having looked both ways a dozen times, I found another break in the traffic and darted back across the sidewalk. My pace outmatched the lady beside me and I internally high fived myself for beating a New Yorker back to Robertson Hall. She, oblivious, continued walking, and I stopped to notice the many inviting brown benches outside of the dorm. A red, black, and white flag hung above the double doors and read Carleton University. I was grateful for it because I had a feeling I was going to get lost in this city frequently.

I pulled my suitcases up the stairs behind me and to my surprise a girl who looked a few years older than me opened the front door and called to me.

"Olivia Jackson?"

How does she know it's me?

"You're the only one missing," she said as if she could read my mind.

Her smile was contagious, and she looked to be surrounded by a halo of light behind her. She beckoned to me, and I touched my finger to the necklace pressed against my chest like I was drawing courage from it, before smiling back and following her into the building.

One thing was certain. Everything was about to change.

BOOK 3 AVAILABLE NOW!

PRE-ORDER BOOK 4 NOW!

Order Your signed copy of Redeemed today!

Order the e-book on Amazon here:

ACKNOWLEDGMENTS

Thank you Jesus for walking alongside me through the hardest year of my life. To my husband and kids, you are my world and I am grateful for your love and encouragement. To Lauren, thank you for being the most incredible friend and holding space for me every time I needed it. C.B. Moore, as always you are the most amazing editor on the planet and I wouldn't trust this series with anyone but you. Esther, thank you for designing the covers for this series. You've done an awesome job and as soon as I figure out how to print tiny canvases I'll send them your way. To everyone who held space for me last year while I quite literally tried to hold my fractured self together, thank you. And to every single person who picks up this book and enjoys it, thank you from the bottom of my heart for supporting my author dreams. If you'd be willing to leave a review on Amazon and/or Goodreads it would mean the world to me.

ABOUT THE AUTHOR

Meggan Larson is an award winning author (best selling on Amazon), course creator, wife, mom, and adoptee. She currently lives in Ottawa, Canada with her husband and three children. Through her indie publishing company, Starfish Stories Publishing, she helps the girl who reads all the books become the woman who writes and publishes them.

She lives her life around the concept of the starfish story, where a woman is tossing washed up starfish back into the ocean as they lay dying on the shore, and someone comes along and scoffs at her. He tells her she can't possibly make a difference because there are thousands and she'll never get to them all in time. She picks one up, tosses it back into the water, and says,

"It made a difference to that one."

Meggan wants to make a difference, even if it's just for one person.

Connect with her at hello@megganlarson.com or at her website at https://megganlarson.ca

Jump on her mailing list:

ALSO BY MEGGAN LARSON

Adopted - Book #1 in the adopted series

Reclaimed: Book #3 in the Adopted series

Redeemed: Book #4 in the Adopted series

The Truth About Forgiveness (non fiction)

The Truth About Finding Joy in the Darkness (Anthology)

The Truth About Success (Anthology)

Being & Belonging (Anthology)

Starfish Stories, An Anthology Volume One

Excuse You? (A memoir)

Portraits (Anthology)

ABOUT STARFISH STORIES PUBLISHING

Starfish Stories Publishing: "Where the woman who reads all the books becomes the woman who writes them."

The Starfish Stories Publishing Company was founded in 2022. Its mission is to create a ripple effect of impact in the world through beautiful storytelling, authentic vulnerability, and inspiring messages of hope and belonging in a world desperate for real connection.

If you have a manuscript you would like us to consider, tap the QR code below and let's chat!

www.ingramcontent.com/pod-product-compliance
Lightning Source LLC
Chambersburg PA
CBHW020333310726
48979CB00015B/2349/J

* 9 7 8 1 9 9 0 4 1 9 6 8 3 *